Praise for Leopoldine Core's

When Watched

"A striking debut collection of nineteen short stories revolving around sexuality and city life . . . Core is a master raconteur and organizes all of her tales around objects and places (most take place in a bedroom or in transit); she captures a quintessential New York cynicism—one punctuated with hopeless romanticism, stress, and hyperstimulation. But the cynicism also produces pure moments of bliss. . . . Entrancing, subtle, and tragically poetic, this collection is an important contribution to queer literature."
    —*Kirkus Reviews* (starred review)

"Leopoldine Core is the author that's turning everybody's heads. These stories set in NYC form an unforgettable work about sexuality, identity, and gender."
    —*Bustle*

"Full of dazzling insight and empathy, each of the stories in this debut will force you to consider how personal identity is impossible to pin down: We are all chameleons, shifting parts of ourselves to make the best of new circumstances. While there is an undeniable headiness to Core's collection, her writing is never heavy-handed: It's refreshing—even bright—and full of heart. This new voice fills a void that, until finishing the final pages, we didn't know was sorely missing. But now that *When Watched* has surfaced, we can't wait for more from Core."
    —*Refinery29*

"Leopoldine Core is one of the most original new writers I've come across. Reading her carefully laid-out sentences is like following a trail of white pebbles through a dark forest of strange insights and passion. Her ardent wanderers exist in the ever-churning flux of their moods and minds, in a haunted, desperate, and bejeweled New York. I get so much from being in her worlds."

—Sheila Heti, author of *How Should a Person Be?*

"Powerful and lucid, these stories are full of pain and sex and the cutting things people say to one another."

—Marie Calloway, author of
what purpose did i serve in your life

"Leopoldine Core writes deceptively poetic prose—there's a delicacy to it, without being precious at all, and it leaves you with a feeling that resonates long after. She captures an essence of her generation, a sort of alienated and self-destructive ennui. I felt so protective toward these characters, like I wanted to reach into the pages and pull them out and save them from themselves."

—Molly Ringwald, author of *When It Happens to You*

"Intent on both wasting and appreciating their youth, Leopoldine Core's distinct and fascinating characters know they're being watched but seldom fully seen. But every now and then, they see each other. And they don't just meticulously observe the sweetly gritty East Village of the recent past; they bring it absolutely to life."

—Sarah Manguso, author of *Ongoingness*

"I love the way Leopoldine Core lets her characters fight toward a turbulent happiness. Like a lesson in how to talk to each other—and also how to be alone. Fast, lucid, and beautifully blunt, these stories cut and swoop to the conversations and meditations that, of an afternoon, can define an epoch in your life."

—Benjamin Lytal, author of *A Map of Tulsa*

PENGUIN BOOKS

WHEN WATCHED

Leopoldine Core was born and raised in New York's East Village and graduated from Hunter College. Her fiction and poetry have appeared in *Joyland*, *Open City*, *PEN America*, and *Apology* magazine, among others. She is the recipient of a 2015 Whiting Award for fiction, as well as fellowships from the Center for Fiction and the Fine Arts Work Center. Author of the poetry collection *Veronica Bench*, Core lives in New York.

WHEN WATCHED

STORIES

Leopoldine Core

PENGUIN BOOKS

PENGUIN BOOKS

An imprint of Penguin Random House LLC
375 Hudson Street
New York, New York 10014
penguin.com

The following stories were published previously in different form:
"A Coffin" in *Conduit*; "Historic Tree Nurseries" in *The Literarian*;
"Smiling" in *Sadie Magazine*; "The Underside of Charm" in
Joyland Magazine; and "When Watched" in *Open City*.

LIBRARY OF CONGRESS CATALOGING-IN-PUBLICATION DATA

Names: Core, Leopoldine, 1985– author.
Title: When watched : stories / Leopoldine Core.
Description: New York : Penguin Books, [2016]
Identifiers: LCCN 2016012621 | ISBN 9780143128694 (softcover)
Subjects: | BISAC: FICTION / Short Stories (single author). | FICTION /
Contemporary Women. | FICTION / Literary.
Classification: LCC PS3603.O734278 A6 2016 | DDC 813/.6—dc23
LC record available at https://lccn.loc.gov/2016012621

Printed in the United States of America
1   3   5   7   9   10   8   6   4   2

Set in ITC Berkeley Oldstyle Std
Designed by Elke Sigal

CONTENTS

WHEN WATCHED

Hog for Sorrow

Lucy and Kit sat waiting side by side on a black leather couch, before a long glass window that looked out over Tribeca, the winter sun in their laps. Kit stole sideward glances at Lucy, who hummed, twisting her hair around her fingers in a compulsive fashion. Her hair was long and lion-like with a slight wave to it, gold with yellowy shades around her face. Kit couldn't look at her for very long. She cringed and recoiled, as if faced with a bright light. Lucy was too radiant.

A low glass table stood before them. Fake potted plants flanked the sofa, their waxy leaves coated with dust. Lucy crossed and uncrossed her legs. Her eyes were quick and green, flitting about the room like birds. She wore a blue mini-dress with a white collar and peep-toe black heels. On her lap sat a chestnut leather purse with a brassy curved handle. Lucy was both plump and long limbed. "A tall cherub," she had once said of herself with a laugh of self-hate. She mocked herself constantly, but with a certain joy. Her joy had a tough edge to it and seemed wonderfully defiant considering the pleasureless nature of their business. Kit was captivated by her. It seemed magical and impossible that one could laugh so heartily while waiting to be handled by a perfect stranger.

At the far end of the room, Sheila sat at a steel desk, staring at the bright page of a catalog, poised with her red pen. She booked all of their appointments sulkily, sighing whenever the phone rang. Kit and Lucy considered her a bitch, though she rarely said a thing. "She does it all with her eyes," Kit had quietly remarked. They spent much of their time on the black couch talking shit about Sheila, leaning near one another and giggling conspiratorially.

Lucy removed a gold-tone compact from her purse and clicked it open. She patted powder onto her chin and gave her mouth a glance. It was pale pink and without lipstick, open slightly, her teeth and tongue peeking through. When her client arrived, she ate a green Tic Tac, biting down on it. He was a short, swarthy guy with a newspaper under his arm.

Lucy rose and clacked across the room with the steady grin of an assassin. It was her third appointment that day but she was an enduring faker, tossing her hair and sucking in her stomach. The man twinkled as he handed Sheila a white envelope full of money, which she counted and placed in a small drawer, then led them to their room with a crabby smile, one hand extended.

Once she was alone, Kit raised her butt off the sofa and pulled her stockings up. Sheila returned to her desk and groaned. She circled something in her catalog and Kit's client called to say he would be fifteen minutes late.

"But he's already fifteen minutes late," Kit said.

"Well," Sheila said, without looking at her, "there was some sort of emergency. I told him you would wait."

"Yeah, I remember that."

Kit walked to the bathroom. The walls were gray with one frosted window and a big beige air freshener that hissed vanilla perfume every ten minutes. She yanked the window open and a great wind came into the room. Snow rushed onto the black tile floor. Kit lit a half-smoked joint from her purse. She kept several on hand at all times in a battered Altoid tin.

She took a squinty suck and held the smoke in, liking the long burn, then leaned her head into the wind and exhaled, snow pricking her face. She peered down at the neon white streets below, car tops mounting quietly with snow. Kit shivered. She took another long toke and thought of the miserable year she'd spent at Bennington, where she had barely attended class, watching snow fall from her dorm window. She had been bored there. All anyone wanted to do was get plastered and sleep around. It was a lot like being a prostitute, she thought, only she had never gotten paid.

Kit took another tug of smoke. She stubbed the joint lightly in the tin and licked her index finger, daubing the orange ember. With one hand, she pushed on the window until it clapped shut, then walked to the oval mirror. Kit stared at herself like a doctor who—right away—sees something very wrong. She wore a sleeveless black dress that she had bought in high school for her aunt's funeral. Her body hadn't changed much since then. She still had narrow legs and a lean, gloomy face, half-moon shadows under her eyes. There was a pubescent look about her, a Peter Pan shapelessness. She flickered between boy and girl.

Kit returned to the black couch, reeking of pot, and began eating a flattened corn muffin from her purse. Sheila shot her a look of amazement and Kit glared back at her. She took another bite of the greasy yellow muffin and a man walked in. He removed his collared black coat and looked pensively about the room, tugging off his leather gloves. "Hi," he said. "I'm Ned."

Kit smiled, her mouth packed.

He stared at her and she tensed with embarrassment, knowing that he was comparing her face to the one he had seen on the Internet, a photo in which she sat posed on the arm of a beige sofa with the stricken look of a woodland creature in captivity. Kit hated to have her photo taken. The fact of one moment being yanked from all the other moments scared her. It was the same fear when people stared at her, much as Ned was doing. Her fear looked fresh and clearly he found this attractive. She seemed unaccustomed to it—unable to hide it—which suggested that she had not been a prostitute for very long.

To Kit, Ned looked a little desperate. Like someone on *Judge Judy*, fighting for old furniture. She watched as he counted out ten twenties on Sheila's desktop, then wiped his nose with the back of his hand. Sheila led them to a square bedroom with scuffed white walls and brown carpeting. Once she'd shut the door, Ned removed his suit jacket and the two sat on the edge of the bed.

"What was your name? Tammy?"

"It's Tonya," she said, crossing her legs. "So what are you into?"

"I'm not going to touch you." Ned pressed his temples. "But I'd like you to get undressed."

Kit nodded absently. Her eyes were bloodshot and her thoughts floated somewhere near the ceiling. Ned leaned his face toward her neck, as if about to plant a kiss there, but instead took a sniff.

"Your hair smells like pot," he said. "And like that big piece of cake you were eating."

Kit turned in alarm. "It was a corn muffin."

He smiled oddly. "You should be careful, eating all the muffins you want. You'll get fat."

"No I won't," she frowned. "Not if I tried. No one in my

family is fat." It was absolutely true. They were a bunch of bean-poles with long feet and sunken faces. Ugly, Kit thought. But uglier was his smile and his warning. His wish for her not to eat. For her to remain locked in a single state of attractiveness, like a woman in a painting, with no body fat or smells, nothing to say.

Kit could smell Ned too. Strong cologne with the scent of his underarms screaming behind it, a bright, beer-like tang. She tried to imagine the women who loved his smell. A wife. Daughters. Possibly girlfriends. These women were lurking in the private lives of even the ugliest men she saw. Ned was neither ugly nor handsome. He had the sort of face that there had to be hundreds of. A pale white oval with a slight shine. Small eyes and a largish nose.

"I bet you drink a lot too," he said, still smiling foolishly.

"Not really."

"Youth is an incredibly buoyant medium," he mused. "What you can do at twenty you can't do at forty."

"So you're forty?"

"About that."

Kit undressed. She lay on the bed with shining eyes, like some dog awaiting the strange and particular abuse of its owner. Ned stripped down to his boxers and stood alongside the bed, staring down at her.

"You are so stoned," he said.

"Not so much," she said.

"Yes you are. You're barely here at all. It's like you're dead."

Kit felt a flash of panic pass through her eyes and knew he'd caught it. Ned was right. She was completely stoned. And because of this, certain things in the room appeared huge. The pink-flowered Kleenex box. The pump bottle of generic lube. Ned's oily, egg-like head.

Kit was arranged facedown on the bed. She shut her eyes

and Ned rocked into the quiet space between his hands. "I think you like this," he said, which was what they all said.

She fell into a partial sleep. Dreamless brown darkness closed around her. She heard her heart beat. It was like a fist pounding at the bottom of a swimming pool. Ned groaned. He came onto her buttocks and she woke, a dull hate glowing inside her. She stood and wiped off her butt cheeks with a tissue. "Are you married?"

He nodded.

Kit returned to the bed. "Does she know you come here?"

"I think she does."

"And it doesn't bother her?"

"She has a very good life," he said. "She's not gonna go and fuck that up." He lay down on the bed next to her.

Kit refrained from pointing out that he had not answered the question. He went on to say that his wife didn't work. She took care of his daughter. He talked about her in a frank and vulgar manner, like she was an animal who had eaten out of the same can for years. He said she was really interested in astrology. He said all women were. He said his wife kept a dream journal and he laughed gently, slightly like a madman. "Who cares about dreams?" he said. "They don't mean anything."

Ned said he was a dentist and Kit wondered how he handled all that revulsion. He complained about his practice and boringly recounted the events of a cocktail party in which he had humiliated a fellow dentist in front of several beautiful women. "That took a bite out of his swagger!" he said. And Kit laughed obediently, which felt like the worst kind of sex.

Kit and Lucy walked to the train at dusk, snow swirling past their faces. The sky was a pearly gray, the moon dimly visible. The two walked along a narrow path of brown slush, bookended by white humps of snow. In their boots and coats, they looked like the children that they were. Each bundled and waddling, their tight dresses and biscuit-colored stockings buried underneath. Lucy wore a long tweed coat with big glossy black buttons, Kit a brown leather bomber jacket and sagging wool-knit hat. They hooked arms, steadying each other.

"He like, reprimanded me for eating a corn muffin."

"What an asshole."

"It was like he wanted me to be dead. Like I was interfering with my potential hotness by living." Businesspeople passed swiftly in black coats. "I hate this neighborhood," Kit sneered. "I hate every single person."

"Are you okay?"

"No. I'm freezing. And I hate these tights." She wiggled with discomfort. "I hate this dress."

"Well," Lucy grinned, "they need you to remind them that they want to fuck you."

Kit laughed. They stopped in front of the train station and looked at each other. "Do you wanna come over?" Lucy asked. There was snow in her eyebrows.

Kit couldn't help but smile sheepishly at the offer because, until that moment, they had only ever spent time together in diners or on the black couch. "Yeah," she said. "I do."

Lucy's apartment was small and lit like a bar, one long room with yellow light in every corner. There was an old claw-foot tub next to the stove and a mattress on the floor by the wall. Kit stooped to pet a brown rat terrier with a silvery snout. He rolled under her hand with a guttural moan, groveling with delight. "That's Curtis," Lucy said.

"It's like a dirty-sock sex club in here," Kit laughed.

"I know." Lucy smiled without embarrassment. "Curtis pulls them out of the hamper. I should probably throw some of them away," she said, lifting a white ankle sock off the floor. "That way I would be forced to do laundry more often." She jammed the little white sock into an overfilled wicker hamper. "I won't go until I'm completely out of clothes. Hate it too much."

"Seriously, I could look anywhere and see socks."

"Do you want anything?" Lucy asked.

"Anything?"

"Well. Beer or water."

Kit laughed. "I'll take water."

"Help yourself, okay? I've gotta take him down." Lucy velcroed a little red coat onto the dog and left.

Kit ran tap water into a Charlie Brown Christmas mug. She roamed around the room, sipping water and snooping vaguely. Apart from the strewn socks, Lucy's apartment was relatively bare. There were tall Mexican candles on the floor by her mattress, a tiny cactus on the windowsill. And on the floor there was an old mint green record player with brown accents. Lucy's possessions looked misplaced, but because there weren't so many, the wrongness of their arrangement had a childish charm.

Kit spotted several photos of a younger-looking Lucy, tacked by the bed in a crooked cluster. In one she sat in an auto rickshaw, in another she stood handling fruit in a marketplace. Kit approached the images intently. She sat cross-legged on the bed and stared up at them.

The door flung open and Curtis raced inside. He leapt onto Kit's lap and squirmed on his back in ecstasy, biting her fingers gently, his wet paws paddling. Kit stroked his underside, her eyes fastened to the photographs.

"He likes you," Lucy said.

"Does he not like a lot of people?"

"No. He likes pretty much everyone."

Lucy hung her coat on a hook by the door. She pulled off her boots and stockings, then fetched a can of beer from the fridge and tapped the top of it with her fingernail. She turned to Kit, who still sat staring at the photographs. "In India I just went around buying things. You can spend a quarter in like a half hour," she said, cracking the can open. "It was so beautiful there. Every single person was doing something. It was such a sensory overload, but way softer than America."

"I want to travel," Kit said. She looked at Lucy. "I sort of feel like I have to do it now, while I'm still cute. Like if I wait till I'm old and ugly it won't happen."

"You might be right," Lucy said and took a swig from the silver can. "But I'm really looking forward to being old and ugly."

"What do you mean?"

"I mean it'll be nice to be left alone. I want to get a little house somewhere with grass out front for Curtis. There's no grass here. I mean, there *is* grass but you aren't allowed on it, not with a dog, anyway. It's like walking through some holy museum." She stooped to pet Curtis. "Sucks."

Kit smiled.

"What?"

"Nothing. I just like when you talk about how much something sucks."

"Fuck you."

"I'm serious! That's always how I know I like someone. They'll be going on about their own hell and it should be tedious to listen to but for some reason it's not. Something about their face or the way they're joking about their unhappiness is so . . . attractive."

"I know exactly what you mean. It's like perfume."

"Right."

Kit set the mug down on the floor and hugged her bony knees to her chest. Curtis trotted over. He lowered his snout into the mug and began lapping.

"He does that," Lucy said unapologetically and smiled at the animal. She knelt beside the record player and put the Modern Lovers on. The record turned and crackled. Jonathan Richman sang *Roadrunner, roadrunner* in his hot, sloppy way and Lucy began to dance, shouting along with the words. *Gonna drive past the Stop n' Shop with the radio on and I love loneliness . . . I love the modern suburban bleakness. I love to drive alone late at night with the radio on!*

"You're so retro," Kit marveled, staring up from the bed.

"I know, right?" Lucy said, catching her breath. "The record player was my grandmother's but all the records are mine." She began to sing again, gaily shaking her hips and shoulders. *Say hello to that feeling when it's late at night. Say hello to that highway when it's blue and white.* Lucy was a silly dancer, but in the way only someone who is confident of their sexiness can be. She flailed about like she had no respect for anyone or anything, whipping her gold lion hair from side to side.

"You're a good singer," Kit said.

"Fuck you."

"I'm not kidding! You're really good."

Lucy rolled her eyes and threw herself back into the air. Jonathan sounded more like a loud talker than a singer to Kit. *I'm lonely and I don't have a girlfriend but I don't mind.* He made her wish she were in a band.

Lucy tired herself out dancing to the next few songs and the two wound up lying on her mattress. They talked about dropping out of college, how it had been the easiest decision in the world. Lucy had studied dance at Sarah Lawrence, which surprised Kit.

"What was that like?"

"It was like being abused. Routinely. By people I had no respect for." She sighed. "What did you go for?"

"Writing," Kit said.

"That makes sense." Lucy smiled. "So when did you know you were a writer?"

"I don't know. About ten, I guess. But I didn't consider myself a real writer. I had one skill and that was to lie in bed," she laughed. "I loved being alone in my room. I mean, that was the real love. I just wrote because there was nothing else to do. It didn't feel special."

"So were you a slow kid or a fast kid?"

"Well I was both."

"Me too."

Kit raised herself up on both elbows and crawled over to her bag. After some digging she brought her Altoid tin onto the floor and surveyed its sooty contents. She returned to the bed with a crooked smile, a joint pinched between thumb and forefinger.

"I can't smoke pot," Lucy said.

"Oh. I thought maybe you just didn't like to at work."

"No, I never do. Some people get all focused and brilliant when they're high but I don't."

"Well I can only focus on like, cleaning my bathroom," Kit said. She lit the joint and dragged on it.

"I can only focus on hating myself," Lucy said. "It's like I can feel every cell and every pore and I'm hating them one by one. Then I put giant signs on them like CRAZY, FAILED, FAT."

Kit laughed and smoke leaked from her mouth. She set the

joint down in the open tin, coughing into her fist. She imagined saying: *I love that you're fat. I love everything about you.* It was the absolute truth. But she said nothing and strained not to look at Lucy. She heard her heart beat. She began branding herself. LESBIAN. LOSER. WHORE.

"So you never get paranoid?" Lucy asked.

"I definitely get paranoid."

"Like how?"

"I just get scared I'll say what I'm thinking or do something insane. Like tell someone what a shit they are or like, assault them."

"You want to assault people?"

"No! I mean, not really. It's just this fear of losing it. I mean, I have that fear anyway. Cause you hear about people doing crazy things out of nowhere. And the slight possibility that I could be one of those people, that someone else could be inside me . . . it's the loneliest feeling. Like what if I didn't know myself?"

"You aren't one of those people."

"How can you be sure?"

"I just am."

Kit smiled. This was one of the nicest things anyone had ever said to her. *You aren't crazy.*

Curtis curled beside Lucy and laid his chin on her breast. She began rubbing his ears and he went limp, collapsing into a state of bliss.

"How old is he?"

"I think five or six. I got him two years ago with my boyfriend. We were totally wrong for each other." She smiled, shaking her head. "I mean, I loved him but we argued constantly." Lucy looked down at Curtis. He was asleep. "I wonder what it's like to hear people fighting in another language your whole life."

"You hear the tones," Kit offered. "You understand. There's probably only one language."

"That seems true." Lucy began stroking Curtis and he roused for a second, then went soft again. "I wish I knew what his life was like before I got him. It's so strange. Dogs are the repositories of stories we can never know."

"That's probably part of the pleasure of looking into their eyes."

Lucy nodded.

"He's very cute," Kit said.

"You think so?" Lucy said in disbelief. "I mean, *I* think so but no one else does. I got him from a shelter. He was scheduled to be killed the next day."

The dog raised his head and yawned. Up close, Kit could see that he had an underbite and one gluey eye, both of which truly were cute.

"He destroyed my sofa," Lucy said and Kit tried to imagine where a sofa could have fit in the apartment.

"That sucks."

"Yeah. He also hates when I talk on the phone. And when I masturbate."

"Oh God. What does he do?"

"He just stares at me with this totally disgusted look and then pouts for the rest of the day. Actually, he also does that when I cry."

"He doesn't want to see you become an animal."

"Exactly."

The next morning, Kit got a call from Sheila. Ned had made an appointment to see her that afternoon.

"I can't believe it," Kit said.

"The corn muffin guy?" Lucy asked.

"Yeah."

"I guess he liked you."

"It really didn't seem that way."

It was Lucy's day off. She padded around the apartment in a short silk robe. Pale blue, with a pattern of multicolored fish, the sash tied loose at her waist. It was a tiny garment, her thighs on full display, a flash of her bum here and there. She made coffee and fried eggs over toast, humming all the while, feeding scraps to Curtis with her fingers. "You can come over later if you want," she said and tucked a blonde strand behind her ear.

"Alright," Kit said, smiling slyly. She squatted in the tub, washing her armpits and vagina. Lucy handed her a pink disposable razor. She opened a window and poked her head out. It was oddly warm. Shrunken gray mounds of snow hugged the sidewalk below. Dirty water dripped from the eaves.

"I can't believe how warm it is," Lucy said.

"And people still say global warming isn't happening."

"Yeah, well, American stupidity is accelerating at the same rate."

Ned arrived in a mute daze. He wore a flat, melancholy expression and seemed barely to register Kit's face as she waved from the black leather couch. Sheila led them to the same awful room and Kit sat tentatively on the edge of the bed. Ned removed his coat and sat beside her. He stared at the brown carpet and said nothing.

"Are you okay?" Kit asked.

Ned grunted slightly. With averted eyes, he rolled her onto her stomach and hiked up her dress. Kit sat up and pulled her dress off the rest of the way, then lay flat on her front like a routine sunbather. She heard his belt fall to the floor. Ned began jerking off and Kit thought of other things. Lucy dancing. The dog. Donuts on a plate. She studied the nicks and scuffs on the white wall, her head on its side. Ned's breath quickened. He gasped and Kit sat up, turning to make sure he had come.

Ned stood naked with his arms at his sides. He was crying.

Kit stiffened. Goosebumps raised over her body. She considered dashing out of the room naked but Ned lurched toward her. He sank his hot face onto her breasts and sobbed for what felt like minutes, then withdrew his face with sudden embarrassment.

Ned moved to the edge of the bed with his back to her and Kit didn't ask what was wrong. She didn't want to know.

"My kid is sick," he said. "Six fucking years old."

Kit said nothing. She eyed the shininess between his shoulder blades.

"I can't see her. I don't know what to say to her." Ned looked over one shoulder desperately, his eyes flashing. "What do you think I should say to her?"

"I don't know." Kit crawled over to him and forced her hand onto the small of his back, patting it. "What does she have?"

"Leukemia," he said as though Kit were an imbecile.

Her hand hardened on his back but she continued to pat him, almost harshly. "It's okay," she said uselessly. "It'll be okay."

Ned turned sharply. "You don't know that. No one does. No one knows what it's like . . . to cease."

Kit removed her hand from his back. She stared into space. "I bet it's like a drug experience," she said finally. "Especially if you're at a hospital and your insides are failing you. Like you probably have odd sensations. You feel really warm or you hallucinate. Then just drift off."

"Not everyone goes peacefully. People die screaming." He had his arms folded.

"You're right."

"My uncle died screaming. He didn't want to die."

"How did he die?"

"Bone cancer."

They leaned back on the bed and each looked at the other's feet. Hers were long and bare. He wore red-and-black argyle socks. Kit looked at them awhile and then through them, at nothing, her thoughts wild. She was angry. She hated Ned for dragging some dying little girl into the picture, for crying all over her breasts. She looked down at her knobby knees, the brown beauty mark near her crotch. *I'm like Lucy's dog,* she thought. *I don't want to see him become an animal.*

Kit considered her own animal self. A wild thing looking out a window. A wild thing made to be a doll. For a moment she loved herself deeply, whoever she was. It was hard to know in the awful white room. She felt as if a circus tent were draped over her existence.

Ned uncrossed his arms. "I've upset you," he said and touched her leg gently. It was jarring and repulsive. He had never touched her this way.

"No. I'm not afraid of death," she declared. "I'm glad the human experience ends. I mean, what if it didn't? What if you were just stuck here forever? That would be scarier than death."

He seemed to consider this peacefully, folding his arms again. "So what are you afraid of?" he asked and a slight smile tugged one side of his face. It was as if he had just remembered she was a prostitute.

"Swallowing glass," she said.

"Why?" he asked.

"Because they can't do anything about it. Glass doesn't show up in X-rays. It just takes one tiny piece and you die a slow, painful death."

"Jesus."

"A bartender told me that."

They were quiet awhile.

"I like that you don't wear makeup," he said finally.

"Yeah. I don't think women should," she said. "It looks so clownish."

"No. Some women should *definitely* wear makeup. But not anyone your age. Makeup on a youngster is redundant."

"You think I'm a youngster?"

"Well you are."

Kit stared at him, glinting with hate.

"Look at you," he said. "Your skin."

"What?"

"It's so *new*," he said and touched her cheek softly, letting his fingers rest there. "Youth is a class all its own," he continued. "You all look alike." He took his hand away. "But the fat breaks down—the *glow*. And you're left with a kind of specificity. You fall into racial stereotypes." He pointed to his own face. "And now you can't tell what I was. I was this beautiful kid."

Kit averted her eyes. She folded her arms over her breasts.

"How old are you, anyway?" he asked. "Twenty-something?"

"I'm nineteen."

Ned smiled greedily. "What's that like," he said sarcastically, "being a teenager?"

"Everyone wants what you have so they try to control you."

Ned looked surprised. He went silent and Kit turned to him, her eyes fierce. "Do you like watching two women together?" she asked.

"What?"

"There's another girl here and if you paid us both double, you could watch us."

"Watch you what?"

"You know."

"Are you a dyke?"

"No. I just think you would like her."

Ned pondered a moment. He got up and reached into his coat pocket, withdrawing a business card. He placed the white card on Kit's bare abdomen and broke into a smile.

Kit saw several other men that day and felt nothing. By nightfall, she stood in the bathroom getting high, staring meditatively out the window. Ned remained in her mind, the weight of his face on her breasts. *He is a hog for sorrow,* she thought. *And maybe I am too.* Kit had never envisioned this life for herself. *This is really happening,* she thought. Any awful thing seemed possible. She was afraid of the concrete and cars down there below, of the opportunity she had always to hurl herself out the window. Kit didn't really want to die, but the fact of having a choice was frightening.

A flood of bothersome memories surged up as she put her pot away. She remembered her mother saying, "Your job should take a little piece of you that you don't mind giving." Kit believed that she had such a job. *It's just my body,* she thought. And it didn't seem like a lot to give away until she considered that it was all she had. *This pussy is my only currency.* It was a sickening thought.

Outside, the moon was huge with white fog in front of it. A twitchy streetlight shone on the hoods of cars. Kit walked carefully over silvery areas of ice. She stopped to peruse the bright aisles of a deli and bought an expensive bar of chocolate wrapped in gold foil.

On the train, Kit sat by the window and remembered that she had offered Lucy's body to Ned and to herself. She imagined telling Lucy this and pictured her repulsed response. Kit broke off a cube of chocolate and sank into a whirling rabbit hole of panic. She almost missed her stop, loading chocolate into her mouth with a fixed look of dread. She walked to Lucy's apartment haltingly, pausing whenever the image of Lucy's disgusted face reemerged in her mind.

Lucy arrived cheerily at the door, barefoot in a black-and-white-checked dress with triangle pockets. They sipped cans of beer on her bed and Kit rolled a joint, which proved tricky since her hands were clammy. She puffed on the loose roll and they talked. Because Kit was nervous, there was an odd theatricality to what should have been mundane chatter. Eventually a silence grew between them. Kit mopped her forehead with her sleeve. She crawled over to her bag and ate the last corner of chocolate, then blurted her proposal.

"And he wouldn't touch us?" Lucy asked.

"No. But he *will* say really degrading things. I actually . . ." Kit stared into space. "I think I really hate this person."

"Why? Because he doesn't respect you?" Lucy said mockingly.

"No. Because he's *crazy.*"

"Look," Lucy said. "Crazy people have one tactic, to convince you that *you're* crazy. So you can't let them."

Kit nodded. "You're right," she said. "I don't know why I even care. It's the weirdest things that bother me about him. Like how he thinks dreams are meaningless." She looked at Lucy. "He thinks his wife is stupid for analyzing them."

"He's probably just a rich guy who went to too much therapy. Those types are really against any sort of prodding of the brain."

In a mock-deranged male voice, Lucy said, "It means nothing. I kill women every night. It means nothing!"

Kit laughed. She considered telling Lucy about Ned's dying daughter but quickly decided not to. She couldn't bear to paint him as a tragic figure.

"If he's paying us double, I'll totally do it," Lucy said and Kit smiled, dropping her head, letting hair fall in front of her eyes.

Later they lay in the dark, Curtis sprawled between them. "I feel weak and depressed from that chocolate," Kit said. Lucy groaned softly, nearly asleep. She had hung Christmas lights on her fire escape and they cast a gem-like glow over the bed. Kit raised herself up on both elbows and studied Lucy. Her plump face in the colored light, wreathed with hair and shadows. Kit held her breath. It felt dangerous to watch such a beautiful person sleep. Lucy could wake at any moment, she thought, and there would be no mistaking the unflinching blaze in her eyes.

Kit lowered her head back onto the pillow. She felt slightly gleeful that Lucy was willing to touch her, even if it was for money. It seemed, somehow, like a far-off compliment. She closed her eyes and Lucy's body beamed in her thoughts. She thought of other girls too. All the girls who'd turned her on wildly and never knew. She rolled onto her side, sweating. Her crotch thumped like a big, wet heart.

Curtis stirred, as if in response to Kit's rising body temperature, the zinging nerves between her legs. He shimmied under the covers and stationed himself between Lucy's feet.

In the morning Kit felt like a criminal. Lucy tromped around in her skimpy robe, Curtis following close behind.

"I made eggs," Lucy said, gesturing toward the stove.

"Great," Kit said, reaching a slender monkeyish arm out for her clothes, which were scattered by the bed, much in the manner of Lucy's socks.

Lucy twisted a strand of gold hair around her pointer finger. "I used to think you didn't eat. Cause you're like, *emaciated*."

"I know. I look exactly like my mom. She's built like a broom."

"My mom's built like a refrigerator."

"Oh come on."

"She *is*."

They were both sitting on the black couch when Ned scheduled their appointment for the following week. Sheila responded with a look of mild revulsion as she penciled it in. Kit pretended to ignore the look but took it to heart. Later on, she called the number on Ned's business card, which in the right-hand corner had a cartoon tooth. It was smiling and had a set of its own teeth. She held the card with her thumb over the tooth while arranging for him to fork over the extra amount in cash. "If you screw us over in any way," she said, "I won't see you again."

Kit saw a number of men that week and avoided Lucy. She paid off one of her credit cards. She learned that Sheila designed clothes when a small green dress appeared on the arm of the black couch. Sheila asked in an oddly sweet tone if Kit would model it for her. She was smiling but a look of scorn remained in her eyes, pulsing dimly. "I need to see it on someone small," she said.

The dress fit Kit remarkably well and she couldn't help admiring it, but this only depressed her. It meant Sheila was something other than an asshole. She was an artist.

Kit bought herself a handsome leather-bound journal that day. She put an aqua mason jar full of sharpened pencils on the windowsill by her bed. Then she tried to write but couldn't.

Ragged stray thoughts circled in her mind. Kit didn't want to sit alone with her life, with the memories of a hundred male voices. She didn't want to fuss over how to describe their faces. Instead she walked around her apartment, smoking pot from a glass pipe with the stereo on. She played Nico, who sounded like a prostitute to her, used and woeful. *These days I seem to think a lot about the things that I forgot to do. And all the times I had the chance to.*

In the morning Kit grabbed the leather journal and jotted down her dream, which felt remotely like a tribute to Ned's wife. She wrote in a panic, the dream whirling and vanishing. It felt deeply important as she raced on, snatching bits of the fleeing dream. Then she set her pen down and read the frayed, mystical prose with satisfaction. It seemed to be proof of something. That she had an inside. *I exist,* she wrote and instantly felt foolish, scribbling over the words.

Next she stood at the stove brewing espresso in a small steel pot, then went straight back to bed and sipped from her mug, a brown-tone afghan up over her shoulders. She watched hours of reality TV, which felt sleazy. *This is the pornography of our lives,* she thought.

Kit wondered if Ned's daughter was dead yet. She hated to think of him sobbing alongside a hospital bed with a little girl on it. *What is the difference between me and her?* she thought. *Between a daughter and a whore? Possession,* thought Kit. *His daughter belongs to him.*

But they were girls in the same sea, she felt. Both their values had been established in relation to Ned's sperm. It was gold when his daughter was conceived. It had taken a long, holy swim to the womb. But with Kit, his sperm had just been trash, just some muck on her ass. It was a weirdly gratifying epiphany. *I am the receptacle,* she thought. *His daughter is a deity.*

Time passed crudely. Kit had several dreams of leaping out of windows and becoming a ghost. She didn't believe in the afterlife but in her dreams it seemed so obvious. Even when she woke, it was true for a moment. Kit was deeply curious about death. *We only know how to go from one place to another,* she thought. *How does it feel to go from one place to nowhere?* Her thinking stopped at the point. She could only wonder. *Death is the one thing you can't write about,* she thought.

On the day of their appointment with Ned, Kit woke in a sweat. She forgot her dream instantly, but felt certain it had been a nightmare. *I was being chased,* she thought. Kit hauled herself into the shower and then got high in the kitchen, waiting for her coffee to brew. She set her glass pipe down and called Lucy.

"What the fuck?" Lucy answered.

"Hi."

"*Hi?* You've been ignoring me for days."

"I'm sorry. I've been really busy."

"Whatever."

They met on the street. Lucy in her tweed coat and a pair of oversized amber frames with rose-hued lenses, her bright hair blowing in the wind. Kit leaned up against a brick wall, squinting. She wore dark slacks and waxy brown combat boots. Lucy removed her sunglasses and they exchanged subtle looks of terror.

"Your eyes," Kit said.

"What?"

"They're so green."

"Oh I know. I get startled in the mirror sometimes. Cause they change."

"I've noticed that."

"The Irish thought they were fairies," Lucy said nervously. "If they had a baby with green eyes, they thought that the fairies had come and swapped it with one of their own." She nodded as if encouraging herself. "So they basically murdered their green-eyed babies—threw them down a well, hoping the fairies would return their human baby."

"Scary."

"I know."

Upstairs they whipped past Sheila and headed straight for the bathroom. Kit changed into her same black uniform and Lucy removed her coat, revealing a silk camel-tone dress with opalescent buttons down the back. She beamed with anxiety. What was pink came soaring up to the surface of her face like a sunset.

Ned sat waiting on the black couch. He wore a gray felt hat with a top crease. As they approached, he removed the hat and bowed his head. Then a foolish smile came across his face. Ned seemed to be mocking the prospect of his own politeness. He was no gentleman and clearly found this hilarious.

Sheila led them to a large room with one mirrored wall and a creaky king bed. The three of them got naked and it all felt very clinical. The room was a bit cold. Ned seemed giddy. It was as if his depression had receded; he glittered temporarily while aroused. He stood alongside the bed and motioned to it until the girls climbed on. "You're an odd couple," he said, waving his finger at them. "One big and one skinny. But that must be part of the turn on." He grinned. "Calm down. I'm kidding."

A pained smile transformed Lucy's face. She was posed like a mermaid on a rock, yellow hair half covering her breasts. Kit made a concerted effort not to stare.

Lucy's kisses were muscular with no feeling behind them.

She broke into breathy counterfeit moans and Kit cringed. Their teeth clicked. Kit felt a bit the way men must feel, she supposed, when they realize that the prostitute they've purchased is miserable to be near them. She wasn't sure why she had expected it to be any other way. *I'm just another creep who wants to touch her,* she thought. *A little creep hiding behind a bigger one.*

Afterward the sky outside was a gray peach. They rode the train to Lucy's apartment with amazed expressions. Once home, Lucy lit the candles by her bed. It was as if someone had died. Kit searched her face for disgust, but there was only hurt. Lucy sat on the floor beside Curtis, mechanically stroking his muscles.

They ordered Chinese food and stood in the kitchen, eating lo mein from take-out containers. Lucy's glazed look of pain dissipated. She hummed and Kit hated her a little bit. For pretending to be unmarked by the last few hours. And by every other terrible hour of her life.

Curtis hopped madly at their ankles. His cries were comically bad, as if a blade were being driven into his body.

"Is he okay?" Kit asked.

"He's fine," Lucy said. "Those are the screams of a manipulator." She scraped brown slop from a can into a little blue bowl and set it down on the floor. Curtis trotted over with a look of slack-jaw joy. He bent down to eat.

"He appears well behaved when he's eating," Kit said.

"Everyone does," Lucy said.

Kit set her lo mein by the sink. "Am I your only friend?" she asked. "I don't mean that in a bitchy way. I don't have any others."

Lucy stared at her. "In a way you are. I used to have a lot of friends."

Kit had never had a lot of friends. But she'd had a few that

she didn't have now. *Becoming a whore is like getting very sick*, she
thought. *You don't want people and they don't want you.* Only she
did want people. A little.

"Ned's daughter is dying of cancer," Kit blurted.

"He told you that today?"

"No. Before. I should have told you. I just didn't want you
to feel sorry for him."

"I wouldn't have."

"Really?"

"I don't feel anything for these people," Lucy said dryly.

Kit reached into her bag and felt around. She wondered
what Lucy *did* feel. Outside an ambulance wailed by, its twirling
red lights passing over the ceiling. She lit a joint and stood with
it burning between her fingers. "I don't know why I get high,"
she said. "My mind is so inherently trippy."

"Maybe you should quit."

"Maybe." Kit let herself stare at Lucy. It was a quiet, burning
stare. Her eyes blazed, pouring with feeling. Lucy continued to
eat, as if she did not notice. But she did.

The Underside of Charm

Ava sat in bed with Gretchen, a woman she'd met the day before in an AA meeting. Gretchen had been sober for eight years and it was her bed, her story.

"The bigger fear was that I wouldn't die," she said with a glazed look, closely monitoring Ava's responses. "It was sick, to manage and control this thing—drinking—like it was God. To prove that I was God over it." Gretchen ran one hand over her tawny crew cut and sighed. It was a story she had told many times, a story she liked to tell. There was the version she told in AA meetings and the version she told to lovers, but both framed her as a macho street urchin, staggering through life swigging from a flask and having epiphanies. She had an aura of smugness, even as she strode across the room to open a window, she bore the expression of someone receiving a compliment and finding it to be absolutely true. Her face was broad and German, olive toned with a spattering of pale freckles. One of her eyes twitched occasionally, a consequence of abusing speed.

It had been three months since Ava's last drink, a vulnerable time. Many warned against dating but she found herself completely pulled to Gretchen: her ease, her obscene self-confidence.

"Do you believe in God?" Ava asked.

"I do."

"And you feel really sure?"

Gretchen paused, tipping her head to one side. "There will always be periods of unknowing. But I think you should let go at that point."

"What do you mean let go?"

"Don't *arm* yourself with belief," Gretchen instructed. "Say I don't know. Throw your hands up. Meet people there."

Ava nodded. "So you go to church and everything?"

"I do," Gretchen said. "Really I go to be alone. It's one of the only private places left in the world right now."

Ava nodded. This seemed entirely true. "I like to pray," she said. "Maybe *because* it's so unpleasant." She began to fidget and looked down at her fingers. "It feels like some humiliating sex act. Like giving a gross guy a blow job."

"Well," Gretchen grinned, "it's no coincidence you're on your knees."

Ava smiled embarrassedly. Pink hues flooded to her cheeks. Since getting sober, she felt skinned, tender as a teenager.

"My parents were atheists," Gretchen said. "And it never made any sense to me. Why put so much effort into slaying something?" She eyed Ava, who appeared captivated. "I've always loved to pray. I feel like something hears my attempts. Not just to be good, but to be *clear*." She assumed a serious expression. "I got to a point where I knew I was gonna die. I remember thinking, *I've got nothing*. All I could do was pray for help." Gretchen brushed some imaginary crumbs off the bed. "I gambled too," she admitted with a distinct note of pleasure. "Actually, I probably gambled more than I drank. It's like drinking but it's all blackout," she reflected. "You're falling right away."

Ava looked past Gretchen and noticed a squirrel on the fire escape, peering from the other side of the glass. She pointed. "Look!"

"Oh yeah." Gretchen smiled broadly. Her teeth were white and sharky. "He used to put walnuts under my pillow. I think I didn't have a screen."

"No he didn't."

"He *did*," Gretchen said, smiling, addicted to her own charm. "The first time I saw him, he looked into my eyes so directly. I'm sure I had a hangover. It was like I was in a cartoon with him and he was the dominant species."

Ava laughed and Gretchen touched her leg. She looked up with a thrill that somewhat resembled terror. Gretchen was calm as a cat, her gaze steady and electric.

They pounced and the two made out athletically, wide-mouthed and groping. For dinner, they had eaten roast beef and vegetables, an oniony dish, and Ava hoped her mouth wasn't the onionier mouth. They stopped kissing and looked at each other.

"Do I have really bad breath?" Ava asked, a laugh in her voice.

"I think we both do." Gretchen grinned. "We could brush our teeth."

"I don't have a toothbrush."

"I have a new one you could use. Still in the package."

They brushed their teeth, hip to hip, and spat green foam into the sink. Both wiped their mouths, smiling. They returned to the bed and resumed kissing. The kissing became a laugh.

"I still taste onion," Gretchen said.

"But mint too."

"Yeah, it's like a little mint messenger carrying an onion."

They laughed heartily and smashed their mouths back together, tugging out of their clothes. Heat came off Ava in great waves, while Gretchen's energy remained cool and mechanistic. A pure chill.

Later it rained. It was a violent fall rain, knocking tree branches to the pavement out front. The two lay naked with the lights on, Ava half under a sheet, Gretchen fully exposed, legs crossed, a pillow behind her back. She got up and removed the screen to close the window. Rain pelted the glass. A clap of thunder lit the room and Ava pulled the sheet up over her breasts.

Gretchen brought a glass of water to bed. She reached for her newspaper and spread it wide in front of her. Another bolt of thunder turned the room white and she flipped her newspaper over with a closed expression. Ava looked around the room. It was sparsely decorated, with a small television, several shelves of graying books, and some free weights rowed by the wall. She felt suddenly, incredibly lonely.

Though she sensed no invitation, Ava rolled near Gretchen and kissed her shoulder, a fearful smile on her lips. Gretchen pulled slightly back and gave Ava a pat on the head, as one would a little purring cat that is bothering them. Ava lay back down and folded her arms in amazement. Gretchen continued reading her newspaper as if she were alone. There was evil glittering in her beauty, Ava observed. Gretchen looked almost cadaverous. She had taken the most ordinary act in the world and injected it with malice.

A pained silence entered the room but Gretchen seemed

unscathed, newspaper in hand. *Charm is a creepy, scary thing,* Ava thought. *The light shifts slightly and she looks maniacal.*

"Do you want me to leave?" Ava said finally.

To this, Gretchen looked up from her newspaper, still naked. She made a face of mock guilt and said, "Well maybe. Yeah."

Ava was jarred. She felt her eyes moisten, if only from astonishment. She considered saying something frank like, "Oh, so you're a *bastard*," but it seemed no use. Gretchen appeared impenetrable. *Responding would be like pissing into a rainstorm,* Ava thought. She got up and dressed, hating to be naked, however momentarily.

"You should take an umbrella," Gretchen said as Ava approached the door.

Ava paused. A smile of acute pain spread across her face. "Thanks," she said and bent down, seizing a small black umbrella with a hook handle. "Bye."

"Bye." Gretchen smiled mildly. It was the smile of a priest or a friendly stranger on a subway platform. *Not the smile of someone who just bought you dinner and fucked you and is now sending you out into a downpour,* Ava thought.

Outside the streets were empty. The umbrella was broken so she had to hold it open. After a couple blocks her arm hurt so she threw it away. The rain had become more of a mist. Ava wanted to drink. But more than that she wanted to vanish, to linger in some way station between life and death. *A ghost,* she thought, *or a gas.*

By the sixth block of walking, Ava was convinced that she wasn't an alcoholic after all. *I'm just lonely,* she thought, *craving some culty community.* She imagined brown liquor in a glass on a wood tabletop and her body softened. It seemed like the most normal thing in the world, to pick it up and drink. *I'm just a masochist*, she decided. *And that has nothing to do with drinking.* It had stopped raining but Ava was soaked. "Fuck you, Gretchen," she said aloud. "And fuck *God*."

Ava walked through her front door and instantly felt disgusted by her apartment: her faded black couch with the broken springs, her groaning refrigerator. She wanted to catapult herself somewhere, *anywhere*. To be in that soft, familiar spaceship, a drink in hand, ice cubes rattling as she raised it to her mouth. Ava peeled her clothes off and let them slap to the floor, thoughts of brown liquor blazing in her mind. She imagined slowly sipping the dark drink, although her drinking had never been slow. Ava had been an Olympic drunk, careening throughout the East Village from bar to bar, shouting things she wouldn't remember. Those nights always ended predictably, with her sprawled under a stranger in a strange bed, tipping into a void-like sleep.

Ava remembered waking up and seeing a stranger's naked backside, their cats walking around meowing. She remembered her dread, her fear of who the person would be when they turned around. *But that was better,* she thought. *Better than all this consciousness.*

Ava toasted a slice of raisin bread and spread butter over it, then took a bite and threw it out. Food was sickening. *I am an alcoholic,* she thought. She ran a bath and tested the temperature with her fingers, hot. She climbed in and wondered if it was possible for someone to drown themselves in a bathtub, holding their body down with pure will alone. *Probably not,* she concluded, *because the creature wants to live.* A friend of hers had hanged himself and she often pictured the act of his departure. The thought she couldn't shake was that, undoubtedly, when he kicked the chair away, he wriggled. *The body fought to live,* she thought. *And while he was wriggling like that, he must have known it was a mistake. The creature said no and the creature was him.* She sank down, her knees jutting up out of the water. *But maybe not*, she considered. Hair raised around the sad island of her face, eyes closed. *Maybe it is possible to end your life unambivalently.* It seemed entirely possible at the moment. With her ears under water, Ava heard her pulse. She raised herself up and stood before the mirror, steam rising around her naked body.

In bed, she wore an oversized T-shirt with palm trees on it. *All I do is talk to myself,* she thought. She wanted to believe that God was glowing inside her. But it seemed that where God might be, there was a batch of whispering goblins, taking turns convincing her of crazy things. The sea of devily voices occupied most periods of silence. They were like her family: menacing and enduring. She wanted to choke them all with booze before one took over.

Ava strained, inside of herself, to tunnel through the dark verbal smog, clasping her hands together. She looked about the room and asked a chair for help. Then the closet door. *Help.* Next the ceiling fan, its slow, maniacal turn. *Help me.* The window. The tree in streetlight, rain dripping off its leaves. *Let me out.*

Smiling

They are lying in bed naked, she with her head on his lap. And he is gently raking her scalp with his fingernails, which she likes very much. Possibly she likes it even more than sex.

"Tell me what you were like," he says.

She smiles and looks up at him.

"I mean when you were little," he says.

"I loved rolling down hills," she says.

"Oh *yeah*," he says, remembering all the hills of his life, high and green and endless. "It was like the first drug," he says. "It felt so dangerous."

"I know!" she says, her eyes growing wide. "There were rocks and shit. It was so exhilarating. It was like sex."

She sits up and they look hard at each other. It is not a penetrating look, though both mean for it to be. Their eyes search each other scientifically, drinking up the exquisite surface detail by detail. Her eyes, his mouth, her nose, his shoulders.

"What were *you* like?" she asks.

"I liked bobbing for apples," he says and grins.

"Oh you did *not*."

"I swear. I was really good at it."

"How could you be good at it?"

"I was really brave."

"I could never get them in my mouth," she says, reanimating the struggle in her mind.

"You have to let them come to you," he explains.

This sends her into gales of laughter. Even when she has stopped, the laughter plays around her eyes.

He touches her face. "I've never liked someone this much," he says.

"Because I think you're funny."

"Yeah that's it."

"No really. What is it about me?"

"I don't know. I think it's your hair."

She shoves him, laughing hard. "Shut up!"

"It's really good hair."

"Come on. I was asking seriously."

"God. I don't know. It's your face. Your heart. Your ass."

She stares. What he has said feels perfect. She kisses his nose and lies on her back smiling, tits splayed. They are quiet awhile. "God," she says, stretching. "I'll never get tired of being in bed."

"I know," he says. "I've never seen such a dedicated person."

To this she laughs and laughs. He joins in, pleased with himself.

"All you do is mock me," she says.

"That's what flirting is," he says.

"I know," she says. "It's a violent act." She thinks of all the people who flirt with her on a regular basis. *They all show their teeth when they smile,* she thinks. Now he is smiling, showing his teeth. She is too. *Smiling is powerful,* she thinks and rolls onto her stomach.

"God," he says. "You have a really great back." He runs his hand over it. This is the first time he has looked closely at this part of her body. They have known each other for only twelve days.

She looks over one shoulder, beaming. "I do?"

"Oh it's perfect." He kisses her spine and she rolls onto her back again, a greedy smile on her face.

He curls beside her, laying his head sidelong on her arm so that his lips are pressed against one breast. "It keeps wanting to pop in my mouth," he says of the breast.

"It doesn't *want* anything," she says.

"Well it's right where my mouth is," he says. "So when I talk it gets in." He laughs wildly, letting the tit in. "It maketh it hard to talk," he says.

"Why don't you move?" she laughs.

"I don't know, I kind of like it." He raises his head and they make out, then stare at each other.

"What are you thinking about?" she asks.

"This."

She thinks he might make a joke but he doesn't. She sits up and pulls a sheet over them. By the bed there's a small stack of books. The one on top has an ugly fish on the cover. Over the fish big block letters spell WORLD'S WEIRDEST ANIMALS. She picks up the book. Under it there's another picture book.

"You read a lot of silly books, you know that?" she says.

"Well you just read *The Metamorphosis* over and over," he says. She stares at him.

"You said you read it every year," he says. "Didn't you say that?"

"So. You *wish* you could do the same thing over and over," she says challengingly, a smile building. It is a playful smile but she means what she said. She thinks it takes guts to do the same thing many times. And an imagination.

"Say that again," he says.

"You wish you could do the same thing over and over."

"Say that again."

"You wish you could do the same thing over and over."

"Say that again."

"Oh shut up." She gives him a little shove. They laugh and laugh, then settle back into silence. She opens *World's Weirdest Animals* and reads.

"Jesus," she says.

"What?"

"Ants of the subfamily *Formicinae* kidnap the eggs and pupae of other ant species, take them home, and raise them as slaves," she reads aloud. "They spend the rest of their lives doing the foraging, cleaning, and babysitting for their masters." She turns to him with a look of deliberate horror.

He grins. "That's pretty fucked up."

"It's just such a *human* thing to do," she says.

"Right," he says. "Humans are way worse though."

"Yeah." She stares into space. "The capacity to organize is endless and that becomes cruel."

He nods.

She puts the book down and he picks it up. "My mom buys these books for me," he says. "Every year for Christmas."

"Oh," she says. "Do you ever buy books?"

"No. I don't really like to read," he says without embarrassment, putting the book back on the floor.

It mildly shocks her, his ease in admitting this, his confidence. "I love you," she says.

"Because I don't read?"

"Yeah that's it." She kisses him squarely on the mouth. "I mean it. I fucking love you. I'm so glad . . ."

"What?"

"I don't know. I'm glad we're dating."

"Is that what we're doing? *Dating?*" he says, smirking slightly. "This is quite a date."

She shoves him, laughing embarrassedly, then climbs on top of him. "You're so goddamn funny."

"It's all fear," he says, feeling her bum with one hand. "It started in high school."

She watches his face as he remembers.

"They were all laughing at me anyway so I thought I might as well take control of it," he says.

"That's smart."

He grins. "I was always making the moms laugh."

"I'm sure you were very charming."

"I *was*. You're laughing!"

"I'm not laughing."

"But you're smiling."

"I *am*," she says, the smile spreading to show her teeth. Then she throws herself down next to him, wanting to see what he sees: the ceiling, mostly.

"It seems like you like being naked," he says.

"I do," she says. "I like how simple it is."

He rests his hand on her stomach and a foreverish feeling flashes between them. She tries to imagine loving him less and she can't. Then she tries to picture herself as an old woman in a rocking chair. She can't. And she can't imagine dying because that would mean the love was gone too.

She wraps her leg around him. She takes a whiff. *Who could die like this?*

Another Breed

"She got the job cause she's good-looking."

"You think?"

"She's a nice blonde from a private school and she probably sucks their dicks."

"*Stop*. I don't think she's like that."

Sasha grinned, sure of herself. "These are men with money. They're hiring blow jobs whether they get them or not."

Cory laughed a little. "You're right." She packed the wooden pipe with weed and held a lighter to the cruddy green, puffing till it glowed. "Men have careers," she said with a gush of smoke. "Women have mouths."

Sasha's grin deepened. "The other day I saw a billboard and I can't remember if it was for cell phones or an actual escort service . . . but the woman was on the phone and she was doing that finger-to-mouth thing." Sasha demonstrated, holding one finger up to a mock pout.

"So?"

"So I was like why do women do that? And then I was like duh the finger's a dick."

"It's like she's thinking about sucking it."

"Yeah or showing you the way in . . ."

Cory relit the pipe and puffed on it.

Sasha held out her hand. "Gimme that." They were sitting on Cory's bathroom floor because it was the coolest spot. Outside it was ninety-one degrees and the whole apartment was roasting.

The two of them looked exactly as they had at sixteen—at least to themselves. They were still best friends who lay around gossiping and looking at the walls. They were twenty-five now.

People often asked if they were sisters, though they didn't look alike. Cory was short with a round face and brown curls that came to her shoulders. Sasha was tall and thin. She had a pointy face and dark eyes that looked drawn on.

"I need a job," Cory said, handing the pipe over. "I'm starting to freak out."

Sasha looked down at the black plastic mouthpiece. It was considerably bite-marked. "You should learn how to read tarot cards," she said finally. "You'd be good at it."

"No. I wanna believe in it too much. I'd hate to be the one making it up." Cory hung her head low, examining her fingernails. They were a little yellow and some were longer than others. "We should both just marry doctors."

"Oh *come on*. Do you really want to be some captured pet?"

"Yes." Cory stared a second. "I'm not a genius like you."

"I'm not a genius. I'm just popular."

"But that's a kind of genius, isn't it?"

"I guess," smiled Sasha. "See? You're a genius too."

Cory suppressed a naked look of delight. She stared down

at the clammy legs sticking out of her dress. "I just need to find someone to feed me."

Sasha rolled her eyes and stood up. "Enough already." She bent over the sink and splashed her face with cold water, then gave the mirror a quick, urgent glance, as if checking to see if she was still beautiful. She was. "Everything costs something, Cory. I mean rich guys are *aw*ful to be around . . . so rude."

"Well they're full of well-being but nothing's ever good enough."

"Uh-huh. Their wives are so . . . you know . . . disposable." Sasha sat back on the floor with a little thud. "I mean disposable if they're *lucky*. Otherwise they just wind up with a rhinestone collar and a long leash their whole life."

"That doesn't sound so bad."

"Yes it does. Those women kill themselves."

Cory leaned her head against the tub. "I'm really stoned."

"I'm not. This is horrible weed."

"I know. It's not giggly weed. It just makes you stupid."

"I don't feel stupid. I don't feel anything." Sasha stuck her finger in the ashy hole of the pipe and poked around. "This is like a dirty old man's pipe," she said and relit the charred little nugget.

Cory cracked up. "It was my grandfather's."

"Seriously?"

"Yeah. I took it from his house when he died."

"That's disgusting."

"No it's not."

"Cory, we're *kissing* your dead grandfather!"

The two broke into high-pitched, chaotic giggling.

"I never thought about it that way." Cory held her abs, catching her breath. "But I guess you're right."

"Stoner." Sasha brought the brown arm of the pipe to her lips and took a long pull.

"You like kissing him."

"Shut up."

"You can't get enough."

"I'm trying to get high, asshole."

Cory doubled over chuckling, her knotty curls grazing the floor. She stayed there for a while, softly convulsing.

Sasha stared at the smeary base of the white sink. "Is it really Sunday?"

"I have no idea," Cory said from under a mass of hair.

"I hate weekends . . . once you get into the rhythms of freedom it's over." Sasha set the pipe down with a small huff. "I'm gonna get going."

"*No.*" Cory's face popped up, flashing urgently. She grabbed hold of Sasha's arm. "Don't leave me alone with the Internet."

"Is the Internet in here?" Sasha smirked. "Is it in the toilet?"

"No but it's where I'll go . . ." Cory stared pleadingly. It was a face beyond tears. "There's this YouTube video called 'Woman Accidentally Cuddles with Burglar.' I've never clicked on it . . . but it wants me."

"Come on, Core." Sasha unhooked Cory's sweaty fingers. "I have to work tomorrow. I just wanna go home and—"

"There's another one that's like, 'Man Trades Kidney for iPhone.'" Cory stretched out on the floor, exposing the floral crotch of her underwear. "Oh Sasha. What the hell am I gonna do?"

Sasha stood up and put her hand on the doorknob, impatient.

"I don't mind being glamorously poor," Cory glowered, "but not so poor I look like white trash."

"You really love this, don't you?" Sasha took her hand from the knob.

"What?"

"You're rolling around in your misery like a pig."

Cory swallowed. "Sorry if I'm *bothering* you," came a dry, splintery voice. She looked ready to cry. "If I can't be ugly in front of you then—what the fuck? Fuck you!"

Sasha knelt beside her friend. "Okay." She sighed. "Be ugly. Be really ugly."

Cory stared up from the dirty tile floor. "Sometimes I have these fantasies where I'm comforting *you*."

Sasha sniffed shyly. "But you do."

"No. You don't need it. You're one of the beautiful people."

"Shhhh." Sasha brushed a fat curl from Cory's balmy forehead.

"I need to be making money."

"Yeah I get that."

"When I meet people I always wanna ask how they do it . . . actually sometimes I *do* ask." Cory's face crinkled up with the embarrassment of a memory. "I'm like an animal watching human life and trying to take tips . . . but it doesn't matter *what* I do. I'm an outsider."

"Yeah," Sasha grinned. "Another breed."

"*Hey!*"

"You know I'm kidding." Sasha smiled sweetly. "The question is how to get paid for being you."

"It seems impossible."

"It's not."

Cory sat up. She lit the pipe and took a grim drag. Now she tasted her dead grandfather. The weed was gone. "I'm a baby and a criminal," she croaked. "I'm picking pennies off the floor."

"Gimme a break."

"If I see a penny I pick it up!"

Sasha rolled her eyes. She helped Cory to her feet and they stumbled into the kitchen, a fine grit pressing into their bare soles. Cory gave one foot a little shake and ducked the strip of fly tape that hung in the center of the room. Sasha raised an arm and fanned her pit. "Jee-sus," she said. "I'm like a fucking chicken in the oven."

"A *fucking* chicken?"

"Yeah. A chicken getting fucked."

Cory smiled a little, then opened the freezer and stuck her arm in. She pulled out a couple popsicles: grape for her and strawberry for Sasha. "This is all I've been eating."

"Shut up, orphan." Sasha grabbed the red popsicle, tore the plastic off, and bit into it.

The two of them walked to Cory's little bedroom, which felt hotter than all the other rooms. She had no overhead light, just a brown skinny-necked lamp that poured light the color of beer.

Cory switched on the fan by the bed. "It'll get cooler once the sun sets," she promised, then opened the window and inserted a bent screen.

They lay with thin pillows bunched up behind their heads, lapping up the popsicles in a quiet, methodical trance.

Once finished, Sasha said, "You could stay with your mom for a while." She gave the wood stick a final suck.

"No way." Cory frowned at the ceiling. "She would just look at me and *know* I was stoned."

"Then what?"

"I don't know. I'd walk to my room, lie down, and drool."

Sasha laughed. "What about typing? You could be a typist. I mean . . . uh . . . a secretary!"

"Do they even exist anymore?"

"Yeah I think so."

"I can't work in an office. I suck at that stuff."

"So fake it."

"I guess I could." Cory's gaze hovered over the limp strands of a deserted spider's web in the window frame. "But every time you succeed in looking normal in an area where you're not, something inside you deadens." She faced Sasha with her violet lips and teeth. "What I mean is that you don't succeed in pulling the wool over someone's eyes without pulling the wool over your own . . . your subconscious goes to the service of public consciousness."

"Then what?"

"You go crazy."

"Jeez."

Cory rubbed her nose. A few different species of sadness were kicking around in her gut now, joining forces. "Every time I consider doing something I don't want to do, I just remember that I'm going to die."

"God, you say it like there are numbers on the wall."

"There *are*." Cory returned her gaze to the spiderweb, which swayed in the muggy breeze like an underwater plant. "I was thinking I could get a live cam in here. People could jerk off to me lying around eating cereal and stuff."

"Who would jerk off to that?"

"People'll jerk off to anything."

Sasha stared. She couldn't argue with that.

"What choice do I have?"

"*Hey.* It's gonna be alright. I promise."

"Please. I'm almost a whore and everyone knows it. It's just a matter of time."

"No." Sasha leaned on her side and looked Cory in the eye. "I believe in you."

"Why?"

"It just seems worth it."

Cory could've smiled or sobbed but did neither. "Am I a needy person?"

"Yes."

"Am I the neediest person in your life?"

"No. You're just the most willing to express it."

Cory smiled. She sat up and noticed her popsicle stick on the bed by her leg. "I just had a popsicle blackout."

"Huh?"

"I don't remember the end of it."

Sasha bucked with a little laugh. Then a breeze came through the window and they both went limp. It was so good.

Historic Tree Nurseries

Frances was fifty-nine and Peanut was twenty-five, and because of this they were often distracted by the looks of others in public. Usually people assumed Frances was Peanut's mother and gave the pair bright, encouraging smiles, happy to see a mother and daughter so glad to be near each other. But then Peanut would give Frances a long, open kiss on the mouth and every smiler would stiffen, fascinated with disgust.

When the two announced their plan to adopt a dog, everyone disapproved. Peanut's friends assumed domineering parental tones. They seemed to suggest Peanut would leave the animal somewhere or forget to feed it. "Plus, what if you and Frances break up?" one of them snorted.

Peanut quietly considered replacing all of her friends with dogs. She explained that she had already paid for the dog, which was a lie. She hadn't even met the dog. He was five hundred miles away, in Marietta, Ohio. He was three months old and his name was Tony. Peanut and Frances had spent hours trolling Petfinder.com and gasped when his small triangle face appeared on the screen. He looked unmistakably like a Chihuahua, but had been described on the site as an unknown mixed breed. The dog had chipmunk coloring, with a dark muzzle and large foxish ears. He was pictured in a woman's dry pink hands, grasped by the torso, with the bratty, oblivious expression of a king's baby, white chest exposed, little orange legs dangling.

Peanut had filled out a ten-page application online and then got an e-mail from Tony's rescuer with more questions. Her name was Gail and she wanted to know everything. Would Peanut leave him alone for long periods of time? No she would not. Was Peanut thinking of moving anytime soon, or having a baby? No, never. Peanut wrote several careful e-mails detailing her unconditional commitment to the animal and then Frances had to do the same.

After an unbearable day of waiting, Gail wrote back. *Alright, I'm convinced.*

"So we're really doing this?" Peanut said to Frances.

"Really."

"I can't believe you're up for driving so far. I've never met someone so willing to go along with my wild plans."

"Some people would consider that a character defect."

"No. You are so good to me," Peanut said and Frances glowed in agreement.

During the week before their drive, Frances flew to San Francisco on a gig with her band, the Invisible Committee. She didn't pick up her phone, though Peanut called several times, leaving lewd messages. Frances was too focused on meeting people at parties, grinning hotly at compliments from strangers. She had a distinct allure, and women of all sorts invited her to fuck them. But Frances didn't want to fuck them. While she developed crushes on various people, their advances often pitched her into despair. Mostly they were fans, beaming with anticipation, waiting for the right moment to corner her. Frances hated for strangers to pounce. It made her feel like *she* was the commodity, not her work. "People wanna bite my aura," she said to her bandmates and they all rolled their eyes. But it was true.

On her last night, Frances slunk back to her hotel room and crawled into bed, relishing the quiet. Frances loved to be alone. She groomed herself ritualistically, flossing before the mirror in a striped robe. She studied her face and then thought of Peanut's face, her bright animal eyes. Frances couldn't help but measure their life-spans alongside each other. *She is like a vampire,* Frances thought. *She is watching a human wither.*

Instead of calling Peanut back, Frances sent her several short, romantic e-mails, which both delighted and enraged Peanut. Some were song lyrics, of which Peanut's favorite read: *I am devoted to your brain and ass and how profoundly they speak. My love is a shaking cup. A little Frenchman.*

Peanut smiled reading the e-mail but afterward felt tricked. She didn't at all like being charmed out of a rageful state and so she willed herself back into anger. Peanut dwelled on the humiliation of leaving dirty messages that went unreturned. She flipped through her notebook, sprawled stomach-down in bed, calves crossed in the air. She loved to read her old poems. *They are like photographs,* she thought. *There's so much evidence of me.*

Peanut turned off the light and lay in the dark imagining she were tough and uninterested in love. Half into a dream, she promised herself she would behave coldly toward Frances as soon as she saw her, which would be the morning of their long drive to fetch Tony.

She had active, colorful nightmares of the apocalypse. Bombs going off, smoke floating from collapsed buildings, people left twitching in the street. Peanut woke up with bags under her eyes. She looked at her phone and, seeing that Frances hadn't called, an old sadness swooped over her. Whenever Frances vanished, it felt like the old days, before their relationship, back when Peanut was still plotting ways to get near her.

Peanut had first glimpsed Frances singing onstage at a bar, leaning into dusty beams of red and pink light, rope-veins running up her forearms. She sang in a low, androgynous voice that broke into little shouts, her manlike mouth almost touching the microphone. Peanut had come to the show with a friend but quickly abandoned this person to make brave conversation with Frances when the next band came on. Frances was friendly and responsive, but ultimately appeared bored. It took months for her to act even remotely romantic toward Peanut, and during this excruciating period, Peanut had talked to herself in mannish tones and masturbated with a galaxy-print sheet hiked up over her face.

On the day of their drive, Peanut sat waiting on her stoop. She wore a sheer, ratty T-shirt tucked into dark denim shorts and white tennis shoes without socks. Beside her feet sat a large straw bag with a rope strap.

Peanut had lived in the same apartment on the Lower East Side since childhood but in the last year, the building had changed hands and since the sale, it kept morphing. First, all of the stone floral ornaments were torn from the facade and then, after months of misguided upscaling, the building wound up looking like a pizza chain with pretensions. Cheap wrought-iron handrails led to a yellow wood door that was often greasy with oil. "It's very Epcot," Frances had sneered the first time she came over. "Sort of a suburban take on urban."

Peanut considered how she might appear waiting on her stoop, bent over her marble notebook, legs crossed, big tortoise sunglasses between forward-falling hair. She smacked a mosquito on her calf.

Frances pulled up to the curb in her olive pickup truck, one arm out the window. She had a skinny, creased face and center-parted Jesusy hair that she kept dirty to darken the gray. "Hey," she said, her voice tender and smug at once.

In the car, Peanut smiled madly. The two held each other and made out greedily for a bit. Then Frances looked nervously out the window, adjusting her black horn-rimmed glasses.

"Oh, come on." Peanut rolled her eyes. "Relax." Her voice had a fluty underwater quality, a subtle echo chamber.

"You come on. You're a sweet little bunny and I'm this gnarly old man. I mean if someone wanted to murder one of us to make a point, they would murder me."

Peanut pointed to a couple of old women sitting on a stoop across the street. They were staring. "Those two absolutely want to murder you. Look at them." She chuckled. "It's like they don't even care that we can see them."

"They want us to see. They want us to know what they think of us."

"Right." Peanut tipped her head onto Frances's shoulder. "That I'm some victim."

"What do you mean?"

"Well you're the old pervert, right? But I'm considered this, like, *idiot child* with daddy issues. Even your friends treat me like that."

"Like you have daddy issues?"

"Like I'm an idiot. They don't really," Peanut paused, "*engage* me. I mean, the level of inquiry is *low*. Like, if we get dinner, they pretend to be talking to both of us, but they're making eye contact with you the whole time. And then you and whoever just wind up prompting each other's monologues. It reminds me of being at dinner parties with my parents as a kid. Back when I was three feet tall and really was invisible unless I was being bad."

"God. You have to tell me when you feel like that." Frances pinched Peanut's midsection affectionately. It was a measuring pinch. A butcher's pinch.

"Okay." Peanut sat up in her seat and remembered that she was angry at Frances. "Or maybe I just shouldn't go. I mean out with you and your friends. I'm not interested in winning anyone's approval." She opened a greasy paper bag full of broken cookies and scones from the bakery where she worked. "You want?" She put the open bag between their seats.

"No. I'm starting to look like a skeleton with a watermelon around its waist," Frances smirked and then dug her hand into the bag, lifting out a crumbly cookie half.

Peanut laughed and poked Frances's hip. "I like it."

"It? That's great. So it exists."

"Oh darling, stop. Anyway, I only took this stuff because it was free. I'm actually pretty revolted by sweets at this point." Peanut began rummaging through her straw bag and pulled out a CD book covered with peeling stickers. She flipped through the plastic pages.

"Can we not listen to the Smiths," Frances said, steering back onto the road.

"Why not?"

"His voice is so endless and droning. It just makes me sad."

"That's the whole point."

"Well, it doesn't speak to my sadness, it *produces* sadness."

Frances reached back into the paper bag and felt around. "What are these hard pieces?"

"Scones. They're sort of awful." Peanut settled on a Gram Parsons compilation and Frances nodded approvingly. "Tell me about your trip," Peanut said in a soft, guarded voice, sliding the CD in. "Dark End of the Street" began to play.

"We stayed at the grossest Motel 6. There was this place next door called Safari, with a big sign listing everything inside. It said, ALL NEW LIVE GIRLS, RIB EYE, BEER GARDEN. I loved that it said *all new* live girls. Like, we killed the ones that were here yesterday. They're in the dumpster. These are the new ones."

"What's a beer garden?"

"I don't know. I think of fat men rubbing beers dangling from tree branches on their naked stomachs. Of course the place was really dark. And the parking lot was full of cars."

"That's so sci-fi. Every man a little king," Peanut said excitedly. "You should've gone inside."

"I know. I wanted to."

"You would have managed to somehow have a great time. You'd have met some *amazing* woman," Peanut said mockingly.

"Yeah and we would have had the most *amazing* conversation. While she was giving me a lap dance."

Peanut pulled the visor mirror down and stared at her face. "Have you ever had a lap dance?"

"I've had opportunities. At Esther's fortieth there were strippers but I resisted. Something about the idea of tons of people watching me get a lap dance."

Peanut imagined Esther under the grinding pelvis of a stripper. She was a rather conceited woman with close-cropped red hair and a birdlike face. She had once strolled over to Peanut at a party and pointedly asked if she was committed to pushing

Frances's wheelchair when the time came. Peanut had been too stunned to say the deepest thing she felt in reply, or even to take a swing at Esther. Instead she had said in a puny voice, "Yeah," her eyes cast downward. "Of course."

"I did go to this place called Debbie Duz Donuts. Spelled D-u-z," Frances continued. "I was in my thirties. All the waitresses there were topless, so me and Esther thought it would be fun. But it was this sad, boarded-up place and all the women looked really grouchy. We were like a couple of mice ordering our donuts. It was like we were supposed to pretend there weren't tits in front of our faces."

"That sums up my whole high school experience," Peanut said morosely. She tilted her face at different angles before the mirror, assessing each pose. "You know your nose never stops growing. It just gets bigger and bigger your whole life."

"Sort of the toenails of the face."

"That's funny." Peanut stuck her arm elbow-deep in the paper bag. *You and me,* Gram Parsons sang mournfully, *at the dark end of the street. You and me.* They rode past shouting boys on bikes. The sun passed behind a black cloud and one hot spot bled through.

"Do you want any more?" Peanut asked and put the hard edge of a scone into her mouth.

"No. I'm turning the corner toward disgusting."

"Anyway it really freaks me out," Peanut said, chewing. "Already my nose is a little witchy and I like that. But in like ten years it'll be casting the shadow of a small building."

"I love your nose. You would look all wrong with a small nose."

"My nose will always be a little closer to you. Like if I kiss you, it gets there first. It's like a dick."

The two laughed and were quiet. Peanut resumed her state

of contempt almost immediately. She hated herself for being so pleasant and pledged not to laugh again. *We'll pay for the love that we stole,* Parsons cried, and a red-lettered sign whipped by. ARRIVE ALIVE. DON'T TEXT AND DRIVE. The words glowed in Peanut's mind. She set the greasy paper bag down between her feet in a quiet rage, the effect of which was oddly pretty. Frances looked over admiringly from time to time. Peanut looked her best when she was pissed. She took on the neat poise of a killer.

"Will you wipe off my glasses? It's like staring through a potato chip," Frances said and took off her black frames.

The joke was met with incredible disinterest. Peanut snatched the frames from her hand, untucked her T-shirt, and rubbed off the lenses. She handed them back to Frances without a word.

Soon they were riding past squat gray shopping centers, one after another, with slabs of dried grass in between.

"God. Walmart looks like a grocery store in a bad neighborhood," said Frances.

"America *is* a bad neighborhood," Peanut said flatly.

"Do we need anything from there? Maybe we should stop."

"For what? A seven-foot box of cornflakes? No thanks," Peanut said with satisfaction. She leaned back in her seat and repressed a smile.

Frances pulled a dry piece of skin off her lip and a dot of blood rose up in its place. She felt anxious beside Peanut, who sat with her arms folded, resonating anger. Often Peanut veered into dark moods without warning and Frances always knew she was being accused of something, though she rarely knew what. She wanted badly to touch Peanut, but knew she couldn't. She knew that in Peanut's stillness, an ambush was coming. "I want to look at you but I can't take my eyes off the road," said Frances. "Whatever look you're giving me, I can feel it."

"How does it feel?"

"Like standing next to a microwave."

Peanut sat stiffly, wishing she could somehow prompt an apology from Frances without explaining how she felt. She bided her time like an animal, glancing out the window at fast-food signs cast with colored light. She felt sharp and focused whenever she was this angry and, in this way, partly enjoyed the eerie mood between them. Peanut visualized Frances in San Francisco, flirting with whole rooms of women, and then settling on one to lead back to her hotel room. The thought made Peanut sweat profusely. Her legs stuck to the vinyl seat, which had split in three places and been duct-taped. She forced her gaze onto passing discount stores, dark casinos with candy-bright signs. Then a strange smile crept across her face. Peanut tucked her hands under her thighs. "So were you a whore in San Francisco?" she asked in a hostile flirty tone.

"Is that what you want? You sound all turned on."

"Come on, were you?"

"No. More of a bore than a whore."

"You didn't flirt with anyone? I mean out of everyone you met, say you had to pick one—"

"But I don't have to. You are always demanding that I do this. It's so demented, Peanut. It's like you're baiting me to piss you off. And I'm not going to. I'm not some dog, okay? I'm sorry to disappoint you."

"I just find it hard to believe. I mean, you can hardly contain yourself at parties. You walk around stroking your tie, waiting for someone to compliment you, and then lean into any woman who shows the slightest—"

Frances shot a glance at Peanut. "Look at you. You're all flushed. You're all jealous and turned on."

"I am not turned on." Peanut straightened her back. "I'm making a point." She stared at Frances with a grim, determined expression. "So tell me who you found attractive in San Francisco."

"Oh my God." Frances sighed. "Okay. Emmet I guess."

Peanut's eyes grew. "Who's Emmet?" she asked in an oddly cheerful tone that Frances knew could go dark at any moment. Peanut was always playful when gathering information about whomever Frances had paid particular attention to. She felt to Frances like someone holding a dagger behind a curtain.

"Just this drummer I like. He's a great guy."

"Well he can get in line."

"What is that supposed to mean?"

"You think everyone's great. And you want to have sex with everyone. Men included, apparently."

Frances opened her mouth to speak but stopped herself. It seemed like a lot of work.

Peanut looked out at crowds of cows in a field. The sun was setting. There was a glare of pink light in the rearview mirror. "What did you want to do to him?" she asked, fascinated.

"Nothing. I don't know. I was just curious. If I wasn't with you I probably would have fooled around with him. He seemed interested too."

"Did you wish you weren't with me at that moment?" Peanut asked sternly, panic flashing in her eyes. "I mean, did you fantasize?"

"It's okay to fantasize. Are you saying you never fantasize?"

"Did you kiss him?"

"No. Not really. I mean, it was a friendly goodbye kiss."

"Not really? Well it's a good thing I ask you these questions because otherwise I wouldn't have a fucking clue." Peanut looked fiercely at her legs. "You haven't slept with a man in over twenty years."

"I didn't want to sleep with him. It was just a vague sort of animal interest. I'm attracted to men all the time but I don't want to see what they become in sex." White headlights whooshed by. "I don't want to be *feminine*," Frances said firmly. "I don't want to be the counterpart to their virility. I'd wind up feeling like some slain lamb."

Peanut laughed, surprising both of them.

"I'm not kidding. I remember going to the butcher with my mom as a kid during the spring and seeing this skinned lamb in the window with an Easter lily in its mouth."

"Jesus."

"It was the early sixties."

"I know that."

Gram Parsons sang his last raspy heartsick song and the two didn't talk. Frances seemed to be controlling the silence between them and this maddened Peanut. She faced the window and cried discreetly, then patted her face with her fist.

Frances felt trapped in the car and wished she were home alone, away from Peanut, her vortex of need. She tunneled into herself and wrote a song. *She's a little biting daisy, tipping into insanity from seventeen directions. Bite. Bite. Bite.* Frances strained to commit the words to memory, hating Peanut for having two free hands and not knowing how to drive.

Soon they stopped at an Exxon gas station and went inside in silence, past glaring truckers with fat guts. Peanut bought a giant iced coffee and jalapeño potato chips. She walked back to the car in a huff and began eating the chips without pleasure, sipping coffee between bites.

A tall man tapped on her window. It was open a crack and

Peanut could hear him breathing. She looked up and a shrill, ex-hilarated look came across his face. He had a brown handlebar mustache and sunburned nose. Peanut looked away. The man was around Frances's age, she guessed, though he had aged differently, with his craggy face and distended stomach. He was ugly.

Previously, Peanut had considered people either young or old. If they were young, there were many stages to consider. But after fifty, she had never bothered to gauge one's exact age. She said *Santa*. She said *old* and looked away. After meeting Frances, however, this snide disregard had veered into complete fasci-nation. She fixated on everyone over fifty. She measured grada-tions of oldness, tracking them on the street. She would see a white-haired man straining to climb a step and want to know how old he was. She would want to ask. To say, "Please, sir, I need to know. Because whatever age you say, I'll file it away and fear that year." She also felt compelled to know the ages of white-haired people who were walking easily in hip outfits, maybe telling smart jokes. Frances was like that, a swarm of energy. She was attractive in her enthusiasm, which seemed unusual. Most masculine women appeared dour to Peanut, as if they believed that this sort of sulky demeanor was maleness. Peanut was too peevish herself to be near anyone like that.

The man with the brown mustache stared at Peanut for a long moment. He scratched his neck, then walked slowly to his truck. Peanut leaned her head on the cool window glass.

Frances had seen the man approach her car. She stood outside the gas station with a miserable look of concentration, holding her dim green travel mug and a bag of pretzel sticks. Frances imagined confronting him. Of course he would think she was Peanut's mother, or maybe her father. Probably he would stare stupidly, trying to decide which. Frances was continually challenged to educate those who oppressed her, to talk openly about her genitals, and because of this she often resisted the urge to confront them at all. Frances found it ludicrous that she be perceived as a parent. She was no kind of parent and never had been. *Harrison Ford really is a father,* she thought. *Possibly even a grandfather, but he will never be called this.* In quiet agony, she sipped her coffee and considered man's eternal separateness from progeny.

Once inside the car, Frances tore open her bag of pretzels and ate several sticks, stealing glances at Peanut, her little foreboding face.

"What did that guy say to you?"

"He didn't say anything."

"I *saw* him. He was standing by the window." She ate another pretzel.

"He just stared. We didn't talk." Peanut said, deliberately aloof. "He had a Bush/Cheney '04 bumper sticker on his truck."

"It really seemed like he was talking to you."

"Well he wasn't."

The sun was almost gone and this made them both feel worse. Frances started the car and looked over at Peanut as they peeled out. "You have crumbs all over your shirt," she said.

"Look at yourself."

In Marietta they checked into a Best Western hotel, which was run by a bunch of smiling Christians.

"So, two single beds?" the blonde woman behind the counter asked. She wore a hideous white button-down blouse with a pink chest pocket.

"No, one king," said Frances.

"It's the same price for two singles," the woman said firmly, still smiling, determined to believe the two were poor and not perverted.

"One king," Frances repeated and the woman's face changed. She was the sort of idiot whose thoughts may as well have boomed from a speaker on her forehead. Peanut and Frances watched her think about them.

The woman stared in amazement. "Alright then," she said, collecting herself, and tensely typed something into her computer. She put a plastic card on the counter and pointed vaguely. "Up the stairs on your right."

Frances wanted to smile. *This is the great thing about capitalism,* she thought. *Christians selling queers a bed. Nothing in the world exists but profit.*

They dropped their bags off and went across the street to Outback Steakhouse. Peanut ordered a baked potato with sour cream and bacon bits. Frances ordered a full steak dinner. She had always been able to eat heartily under stress and Peanut found this unattractive, too warlike.

Peanut slouched, letting her long brown hair fall over one eye. Lewd, tawny light lit the exposed half of her face. "So you're not going to talk to me?" she asked, pissed to be the first to speak.

"You aren't saying anything either," Frances said impassively.

"Well, I don't know what to say to you when you act like this."

"What, like mean?"

"More like heartless. Like a piece of statuary." Peanut stared at Frances. "It's like you're autistic."

Frances smiled like a wolf. "Do you know what that means? To be autistic?"

"Of course I do. Don't quiz me."

"Just tell me what you think it means."

"It means someone who can, you know, rattle off all the prime numbers, but not, like, say hello."

Frances chewed her steak and swallowed. "I'm like that?"

"Yeah."

Frances was surprised by how much this hurt her feelings. She continued to eat and wanted to cry.

"I just wish you would speak," said Peanut. "You could say anything."

"No," Frances snapped. She set her fork and knife down. "You want me to say something *specific*. You want to have a conversation where you write both sides, like a play."

Peanut looked at her potato and wanted to shriek. It was true that she often staged conversations with the hope of eliciting particular responses from Frances, but for this she felt no remorse. It seemed to Peanut that Frances didn't know how to talk to people. She could be unduly frank, accidentally mean. She needed help.

On the table in their hotel room there were cheap butter cookies in a plastic wrapper. Beside them a card read, *To Our Guests: Because this hotel is a human institution to serve people, and not solely a money-making organization, we hope that the peace of Jesus Christ will rest on you while you are under our roof.*

"You believe this shit," Frances muttered. On the card she wrote: *This is actually really offensive to Jews and Muslims,* then sat in a maroon chair and ate both cookies.

Peanut was too tired to maintain her cold exterior. She turned on the television and took off all her clothes, then poured herself stomach-down into bed.

Frances apologized from the maroon chair, though she

still didn't know entirely what for. She walked to the bed and stood there.

White sheets covered Peanut's ass and legs. Blue TV light blinked on her back. She peered over one shoulder to see Frances's expression and then put her face back on the pillow.

Frances sat on the edge of the bed and stroked her head and back carefully, as if she were touching a terminally ill animal. Peanut's mouth fell open. She let out a little groan, loving to be touched this way, like she was sick and precious. She cried in a small way that soon opened into a breathy sob.

Peanut was flipped over and explored. She continued to cry and it felt fantastic. Between gasps she explained that the last few hours had been lonely. "And you should have called me back in San Francisco."

Frances nodded sincerely. She was moved to see Peanut cry.

Peanut wiped her face with her fist and sat up, relieved enough to notice how uncomfortable she was. "I hate a tucked sheet," she said and began tugging the sheets loose.

"I like it tucked."

"I like one leg out."

"Well, you'll like menopause then. That's all it is. One leg out all the time."

Later the two lay naked in bed, idly touching each other's bodies, lights out.

"You sound like you're crying when you come," said Peanut.

"That's so embarrassing."

"No, I like it. It actually sounds somewhere between crying and laughing."

"You sound like a puppy being rolled off a cliff."

"No I don't," Peanut laughed.

"You do. And your back tenses. It has this great indent like an ass or a peach. A long peach." Frances held Peanut's jaw. "Please spend the rest of my life with me."

"You mean our life. Spend the rest of *our* lives together."

"No, my life. I mean, yours will go on after mine," she said in an oddly casual way, as if she was talking about someone else's death.

"You don't know that," Peanut said and a restrained sob entered her voice. "I mean, there's no way of knowing that."

"It's easy to assume."

"I could become very sick. Maybe I'm sick right now and it's invisible for the moment."

"I bet you aren't."

"Or what about that volcano? It could cause a global holocaust." Peanut took a breath. "I think about you dying all the time and it feels so stupid. I mean, I'm basically stunned the world isn't over. It could end any day. So why, you know, dwell on any moment beyond this one?" She made the monstrous near smile of someone about to cry, and then squashed the expression on Frances's shoulder. Peanut stayed there for a moment and then withdrew her face with a great breath. "When people make plans to, you know, meet someone their own age and get married and have a baby and then, I don't know, have some synchronized death, it just seems like this denial of what we know to be true about life. That it ends. And we can never know when."

"So you never wish I was younger?"

Peanut was startled by this question. *"No,"* she insisted, putting her hand on Frances's flat chest. "I'm in love with you now. But sometimes I want to meet the other yous. Like, I want to hang out with you in 1970. I want to meet *her.*"

"I love you from 1970. I love you from all points in my life,"

Frances said, moving her knuckles over Peanut's stomach. She wanted to stay awake forever, to never let go. Frances hated the vulnerable moment before sleep. She felt she might drop right into death.

Peanut sat up, moonlight from the window pouring on her face and shoulders. She stroked the backs of Frances's legs, saying "darling" again and again, all the while dwelling on thoughts of a world without her darling. It was hideous to contemplate.

Peanut thought about time travel. How could she not? She thought about wormholes and machines from science fiction movies, all the magic that could save them. *If only time were stretchy,* she thought, then her sense of time could be sped up and Frances's could be slowed down. She felt embarrassed thinking this way, but also entitled. Because everyone else had it wrong. The problem with their relationship wasn't moral at all. It was biological. It came down to the bodies they happened to have and the looming fact of death.

In the morning Frances woke up before Peanut. She got dressed and brushed her teeth and stood before the bathroom mirror, staring at her face. The white overhead light was bad and she found her appearance a shock. Frances didn't feel like the person she saw. She didn't feel *old.* She had always identified herself with her body's powers and saw that they were slipping away. So who was this other person? Frances considered the assembly line of existence and one thought looped in her mind. *I'll die too?*

Peanut walked in naked and sat on the toilet to pee.

"I look like some rotting Keith Richards," Frances said.

"You are so vain."

"I know." Frances poured oil from a skinny brown bottle

into one hand and worked it through her hair. "You know what the worst thing about aging is?"

"You're always telling me what the worst thing about aging is. I've heard like sixty worst things."

"Well, in the moment it always seems like the worst thing."

"Okay, so tell me."

"Eyebrows. I keep looking at pictures of myself and thinking what's wrong with my face? *Oh*, I have no eyebrows. And there's nothing to be done! You know, straight women start to pencil them in but that looks really freakish."

Peanut flushed and stood up. "I have this weird dark hair on my stomach." She pointed to her abdomen. "I pluck it and it grows back."

"Well I have, like, an eight-foot whisker coming out of my neck."

Peanut walked over to Frances, examining her. "It's barely noticeable. And anyway that's normal. It's an aging thing. But I shouldn't have stomach hairs."

"Well, you know, your friends have probably already told you this, but it's *contagious*."

Peanut smiled and kissed Frances's ear. "Darling, you're completely hot," she said and hugged her from behind, clasping both hands over her chest. "I chased you, remember?" she said. "You didn't even like me."

Frances grinned. "It wasn't that I didn't like you. I just thought you were so young. I mean, you seemed like an absurd candidate for my love."

Peanut knelt on the floor and turned Frances toward her. She kissed her knees, then held them like apples and looked up triumphantly.

Frances laid her hand on Peanut's warm head. "Baby, you're such a dirty opportunist."

After checking out, Peanut and Frances asked an unfriendly man in the parking lot to take their photo. It turned out he was just European, which they later laughed about. He took five pictures, each at the wrong moment.

"I look increasingly like a leprechaun," Frances reflected as they scrolled through the pictures on her digital camera.

"Well, I look pale and crazy. Like I've just been let out of an institution for a little sunlight."

The last photo was the worst. They exploded into a fit of laughter.

"Jesus. I look like some gnomish version of Iggy Pop!" Frances cried.

"You do! And look at *me*. I love how deliriously happy we look. Like we have no idea how ugly we are."

They drove up dirt roads, past dilapidated farmhouses with brown chickens patrolling out front. As directed by Gail, Frances stopped at the last green shed and parked under a tree.

They began walking and approached a dark barn with a beaming tin roof. Rusted farming implements lay sunken in the earth out front. Peanut pointed to a group of black-spotted pigs, lounging in the sun with drunken looks. She put her hand over the chicken wire and they came running, leaning their genital-soft snouts to her fingers. "Pigs are very smart," Peanut said, stroking one on the face. "Smarter than dogs. And toddlers."

Frances stared at the pigs. "Maybe we could have one someday. And a horse," she said. "Life doesn't seem long enough."

"It isn't," Peanut smiled.

They walked on, past staring goats. Over raised roots, green weeds shooting up around rocks. The two stopped at a dented aluminum mailbox on a wood post. They walked up the gravel drive and through a high metal gate.

Barking dogs came bounding toward them. Gail stood from a plastic chair on the porch, waving. She wore a collared peach dress with square front pockets and a dirty beige visor. A barking spaniel leapt at her feet, nipping the hem of her dress. "Gladys!" she said sharply. "Cool your jets."

Peanut spotted Tony immediately among the pack, trotting their way. A bright fox with dark, wet Disney eyes, pink tongue out.

Gail shook hands with them. She looked wind-beaten and suspicious. Frances recognized her hands from the photograph on Petfinder.com.

Tony began rolling on the grass and Peanut knelt, following him with her hand. He lay submissively for a moment, accepting a stroke, the sun in his orange hair. Then the dog stood on his skinny hind legs and licked her fingers ecstatically.

Gail stared at them. A wide grin spread across her face. "He's cuter than in pictures, huh?" she said. He was. Peanut rubbed his rabbit-soft chest in awe, his heart beating so close to the surface.

Gail warned that Tony would cry for a few days and they nodded, their eyes fixed on the animal. "I like pictures," Gail said. "Send pictures of him." She handed Peanut a record of Tony's vaccines and a ziplock bag full of brown kibble, then a little blue harness and leash.

Peanut gave Gail a check and lifted the puppy up into her arms. "Oh my God," she said, beaming. It was the gentlest weight, like a small bag of flour.

Frances stroked the dog's face with one finger. "I know."

In the car Peanut held the dog with both hands and wanted to write. Black birds flitted by and she let herself forget the poem growing in her mind, which felt wonderfully wasteful, almost decadent. *What kind of radio is a bird? How do they know where to go?* Peanut grasped the dog in a tranquil daze.

"You look like you just gave birth," said Frances.

"I feel like I did."

Frances glanced at Tony. "He seems like a serious little guy."

"He does."

"What fine career could he have where no one would notice he was a dog?"

"Shrink?"

They laughed and laughed.

"He could have an assistant explain all of his intentions," said Frances.

"He wants you to take him for a walk," Peanut joked.

They passed long, low humps of grass, gray trucks like a train of elephants. And a green sign that read HISTORIC TREE NURSERIES, EXIT 41, with no explanation. Both thought of what this might mean. Peanut pictured people kneeling to water rows of tiny baby trees. Frances thought of dioramas of people planting trees in the past. The dog began to cry. It sounded like he was being burned with cigarettes. Then he rolled onto his back and looked up distrustfully, his bright white chest thrust forward like Christ. "Chihuahua on a cross," Peanut cooed in a mockingly piteous voice.

"That sounds like a band name."

"We should claim to be in that band. Like when people think you're my mom, we should say no, we're bandmates."

"That's so great." Frances cocked her head in thought.

"Because I really hate making a point of saying you're my girl-friend. People always wind up looking ugly when they try to make a point." She took one hand off the wheel to touch Peanut's leg. "Our first album could be called *Frantic Licks*."

Peanut roared with laughter. "You know, darling, you look a little like a dog. Because you are kind of always smiling. And you smell like a dog. In a good way."

"I think I was a dog."

"No, you *are* a dog." Peanut looked out at the wide road, the white light beaming on car tops. She patted Tony. "You don't really believe in reincarnation, do you?"

"Well, not really but it's very appealing. I sort of entertain it, with past lives and stuff. Like, my mind slips into it meta-phorically. You never think about having other lives?"

"No."

"So you think people die and then just return to static."

"No, they return to nothing."

They passed lush green farms, black cows in profile on the crest of a hill, a dead deer arranged with its bottom facing the road. Tony's cries were reduced to a croaking whimper and then, in grim acceptance, he tucked his snout between Peanut's knees.

They weren't at all hungry but figured they should eat. Frances took the next exit and pulled over. They sat on a skinny plot of grass in the shadow of a taco chain. Tony peed reluctantly, tugging at his leash.

Frances bought nachos and they ate cross-legged on the grass, holding the cardboard boats up in front of their mouths, away from Tony.

"He has the build of a piglet," said Frances.

"A pig in a fox costume."

"A very clever pig who didn't want to die."

The dog stood on his back legs with a desperate expression, begging for all the things he smelled. "Look at him," Peanut said, smiling.

"Dogs are so more apparently animal than us that we get to laugh at their desires," Frances declared. Peanut agreed. They wiped their mouths and held each other. They looked down at the dog, their tiny witness. He lay stomach-up in the grass.

Frances stroked his throat. It occurred to her that she could die around the same time he did. The thought was a shock and then felt sort of funny. She smiled at the animal, the little measure of his life. *A nano life that matches the end of me,* she thought.

Frances put her hand on Peanut's shin. They both looked down at the hand and then, sensing that people were staring, Frances withdrew it and looked up.

They were surrounded by teenagers with benign, captivated expressions. Wives grabbed their husbands by the arm, pointing gleefully. A little boy stepped forward and shyly asked to pet the dog.

Never before had the two been so tenderly observed. They looked at each other and then back at their audience, alarmed. Strangers stood patiently, all lit up, beside a single gnarly tree. Tony tilted his head, ears erect. He studied the crowd and they crept forward. Everyone wanted to touch him. Everyone beamingly asked, "What kind of dog is that?" instead of "What the fuck are *you*?"

When people left, new strangers appeared. Some stood at an arm's length and they were radiant, waiting for their pleasure. They seemed to be touching the dog even before their hands had landed. Tony offered his underside and stared up seductively. He had an appetite for everyone. The dog was littleness itself and this was his power. People weighed him in their hands. They pointed out his smallness repeatedly, almost to the point of chanting, as if Peanut and Frances were in denial of the dog's size and needed to be convinced. "He's a tiny baby!" a young girl blurted.

This is what it means, Peanut and Frances realized, to be the keepers of something beautiful. This is what it means to become other people. They thought about what they had been when they stood next to each other. Freaks, strutting their base interests. But now, next to the dog, they lost their queerness, if only for a moment. "We're sort of like Elvis's family," Frances whispered. "The trash these people are willing to put up with to get to the king." Tony shot them a long look, as if in agreement, and stepped out into an area of sunlight. He was more aware of his beauty than any creature they had ever met. Everyone crawled around him. They sat in the sun, fondling his warm velvet head. And he shined.

Chubby Minutes

She sees him at the grocery store. He doesn't see her. He is with his daughter. He is putting green apples in a bag.

She grabs a pear and pretends to examine it. She puts it down. She walks over to the melons and stares abstractedly, her heart hammering. She looks up and he's smiling at her. His smile is warm. Instantly she feels weak and excited. He is walking toward her now.

"Hi," she says.

"Hi," he says. He's standing right in front of her. She's looking down.

He is divorced now so technically it's possible that they could date. *Or just have sex,* she thinks. She can't think about him without thinking about sex. And so she is afraid to look into his eyes, afraid he will know and be disgusted. *A man likes a woman to be ambivalent,* she articulates in her mind. And she has never been ambivalent about who she wants to fuck. She has always been sure and she thinks that certainly there is nothing uglier than this, a woman who is sure.

They both ask how the other is and both say, "Good." Clearly both are lying.

She tries to control her face. "I don't know how to pick melons," she says.

"You've gotta look for the pecks," he says.

"The what?"

"The pecks," he repeats. "Birds go for the sweeter ones."

This makes her blush. What he said feels lewd, filthy. *But it isn't filthy*, she thinks. *It's me. I'm filthy.*

She looks down at the little girl, who must be seven by now. It is a knowing face. A face that knows she is filthy. "Hi, Becky," she says to the child, who says nothing.

"She's a little shy," he says, patting the girl on the head. But shy is the wrong word. Becky looks suspicious. *Little girls know everything*, she thinks.

"Well," he smiles again. "It was nice running into you."

"Yeah." She cannot believe their encounter is over. She hates the politeness of her life. He walks away.

She shops impatiently. She cannot bear the fact of time. How it keeps passing. How she has to wait to pay for cans of soup, to have sex.

She wants the man to know what she knows, that she wants him. And somehow she feels that he already does. She has fantasized so heavily and for so long that she feels her fantasies hold a kind of penetrative power. *It's as if my daydreams have hacked into his*, she thinks, her eyes shining. She feels certain that she has appeared in his thoughts. She has been naked in his thoughts and this same naked body has returned at particular hours of the day. *Possibly we are having the same fantasies at the same exact moments*, she thinks, which makes all the dullness between them in public seem coy and silly.

She walks to her apartment and passes a couple. All she hears the man say is "There are two types of people," and instantly she hates him.

On her stoop there is a group of drunk teenagers smoking cigarettes. "You can't sit here," she announces, clutching her brown bag of groceries. "You have to leave."

One woman says "Cunt," under her breath. Another says "Bitch," loudly. They all leave and she puts her key in the lock. *I used to smoke cigarettes,* she thinks, moving into the building. *I used to be a teenager. Now I'm a Bitch and a Cunt.*

Upstairs she gives herself an orgasm. The sun is setting. The window is open wide. Red light pours over the room. She rolls onto her side and imagines the man and his daughter eating dinner. She thinks that she would be happy just to fuck him once. She thinks that it isn't true what people say about men, how they are dying to fuck all the time. She thinks that men are in fact a little prudish, hard to get in the sack.

She reflects, though, that she wouldn't be happy to fuck him just once. She loves this man. And if they fucked she would say it. Almost against her will, she would say, "I love you." She pictures him saying it back. "I love you. I've always loved you." Then his face disintegrates.

She grows anxious. She thinks of all the pressures assigned to a person who is loved. She thinks that certainly if he loved her, it would be because he didn't really know her. It would be because she was hiding certain hideous qualities. And it would only be a certain amount of time before these qualities surfaced. Soon he would know that she couldn't drive. He would also know that even while walking or riding her bike, she often had no idea where she was going. He would know that she couldn't give directions to tourists. *He would make fun of me,* she thinks and cries a little.

He would also discover that she had no urge for cleanliness, that in fact she must force herself to clean her apartment. That when she does not force herself, the kitchen quickly gets filthy, with mice walking idly across the counter, like it is their home. And the truth is that she doesn't really mind it this way. *If I never had anyone over,* she thinks, *it would always be filthy.* She is amazed by people who clean compulsively. These people happily call themselves freaks and she hates them for it. Because she knows who the real freak is: the slob.

There is also the issue of her body. If he loved her it would be because he hadn't seen all of her. It would be because they had fucked in a certain dim honeyed light the first few times. Then, gradually, as they fucked more and more, he would start to notice all the small ugly things. And with each discovery he would stare in silence, weighing his love against the new offense.

She wonders if Becky said anything to her father after they walked away. She wonders if Becky said, "That woman is weird," or simply, "I don't like her." These visualizations produce panic. It seems to her that a lot of men care what their children say these days. It was not like this when she was a child. Her father preferred when she did not speak; and often when she did speak, he would act as if she had not, humming to himself.

I was a child so long ago, she thinks. She thinks that it isn't true what people say about time, that it's fast. Because time has felt fat to her. Every minute has been like a steak passing slowly through space. And she is tired. Tired of wading through the lard of her lifetime, the minutes and the hours.

She thinks of the man on the street who said, "There are two types of people." She still hates him. She hates the way people in her neighborhood seem to lecture each other on dates. But she thinks now that the man is right, there *are* two types of people.

There are the people who wake up afraid, she thinks. And her mother is this way, puttering around nervously at seven a.m. *Then there are the people who are afraid at night. Afraid to sleep.* She is this way.

It's not her creaking ceiling that she fears or the shadows that have begun pooling on the floor. Because she is no longer in the room. She's in a canoe with a hole in it. She watches the water pour in and realizes she's dreaming. Then she wakes herself up, jerking with a snort.

This happens several more times. She wipes the drool from her mouth. *Why won't I let myself dream?* she thinks with a chill. She senses, as she has sensed before, that there is something she doesn't want to know about herself. Something that the goblins of her subconscious know.

She rolls onto her side. With one ear pressed to the pillow she can hear her heart beating. The more aware of it she becomes, the louder it gets. And time is waddling by. The minutes are chubby and endless.

She decides that she would be a whole other person if the man were there beside her. She would be serene, weak and pink with sex. The air between them would sing as they stared at each other. And when the light went out she would not lie awake. She would sleep.

The Trip

"You're going to miss that faculty dinner," Susan said to Henry and he frowned in agreement. The van was packed, but two days later than planned. It was Thursday and they were finally pulling away from their Tribeca home and heading to Missoula, Montana, where Henry had been invited to teach poetry for the semester.

Susan looked out her window at the bright winter sky. "We packed too many books," she said.

"That's good. We might become other people," Henry said—already he was speeding. "And who knows what *they'll* want to read."

Susan hummed appeasingly. She was a poet too, but she wouldn't be teaching that semester. She planned to write.

Both of them had heard such wonderful things about Missoula, how the mountains looked purple just before sundown and choirs of coyotes sang into the night. But the hell of packing had sapped much of that first excitement. The drive would take at least three days and already they were exhausted.

Henry yawned. He had just turned seventy. He had a long face, a thin, constant grin surrounded by stubble. He wore thick black rectangular specs and a plaid wool button-down with a moth hole near the collar.

Susan leaned her head on his shoulder. She did this all the time.

Henry had thin, puny shoulders and Susan's head was heavy. But he had never in all their forty-two years said so. He was just glad it was *her* head. Out of everyone in the world, Susan was the one mucking around in his life, routinely pissing him off. *It could have been a lot of other women,* he thought to himself, a few females spilling through his mind. *Nope.* It was Susan! Of course it was.

Like magic Susan lifted her head off his shoulder and stared out the window. Henry glanced at her and grinned. At sixty-six, Susan had become thinner—more frail, with bright streaks of white in her hair. *What would I do without her?* he thought, knowing full well that this sort of thinking was a two-headed beast. Just as he was quietly loving her, he was also manipulating himself into it. But he didn't mind. The love came.

Henry pulled into the first gas station he saw and a pimpled attendant in a red vest walked up. The guy stared, then tapped on the glass. Henry rolled down his window. "Yes?"

"You know we have full service," the guy said, pointing.

Henry cut his eyes and stared. "Yes I do know that."

"Okay." The guy shrugged and walked away.

"Ageist little twerp," Henry said, rolling up his window. "I can *walk* for Christ's sake."

"People have treated me like that my whole life," Susan huffed. "Always assuming I need *help*. Now that you're old you're getting a taste of what it's like," she said with a wry smile, "to be female."

"Who's old?" he said, thumbing the screen of his phone. He saw an icon of a snowflake and paused for a few seconds, not quite registering the little picture.

"If I'm old then you're old," she said. "And I *am* old."

"Nonsense," he said and gave her a hard little peck on the cheek. "You're my spring chicken. My honey bunny."

Back on the road Susan pointed to some graffiti on a billboard. Huge, cloud-like letters spelled something, though she didn't know what. It may as well have been in another language. "God," she marveled. "I can't believe someone actually stood up there and wrote that. It's so *high*."

"That's why I'm not worried about someone cleaning our windows," Henry said. "It's probably the same people."

Susan opened a bag of black licorice and reached in. She eyed the speedometer. "Slow down, will you *please*? You're making me sick."

"Al*right*," he said as if she had already asked him many times. He relaxed his foot on the gas pedal, bringing the needle down only slightly.

"I wish we could take a train there," Susan said, chewing the candy. "Trains put me right to sleep."

Henry glanced at his wife. "In Russia you can't sleep on trains," he said.

"Why not?"

"You wake up without organs."

"Henry."

"Either your kidney or your liver. *Gone.* I think the demand for livers is higher than—"

"Henry, please."

"The future has been here for a long time," he said in a kind of trance. "We're not even people anymore."

"That's *enough*," Susan said firmly. But it was too late. Her mind already contained a sloshing cooler of organs. She set the bag of licorice down in the drink holder, feeling nauseous. "You know what I find really disgusting?" she said. "Harvesting."

"Oh I *know*," Henry said, nodding adamantly.

"Just the thought of someone's organs kept alive . . . without them."

Henry made an empathizing hum.

Susan tilted her seat back and arranged her scarf over her face.

When she woke, Henry was outside pumping gas. It was dark and a light snow had begun. The grass looked slick.

"We should stop," she said when he got back in the car.

"It's not so bad," he said. "I have another hour in me at least."

But when Henry got back on the road, they quickly had the sensation of gliding over water.

"Henry," Susan said in a clipped tone. "We have to stop." Snow was falling heavier by the second.

"I know."

"Take this exit."

"I *know*," he said, turning off the road. The car swerved slightly and he braced the wheel, struggling to complete the turn.

"Henry!"

"Shut up for a second."

"You're going too fast!"

A bright Holiday Inn sign appeared at the roadside, behind it a beige castle nestled in darkness.

"Thank God," Susan said but the tawny offering whipped by. "For Christ's sake! Why didn't you *stop*?"

"It looked expensive," Henry said quickly, though in fact he was afraid to make the turn. "There's another one coming up I think."

Now they were driving down a thin road flanked by the tall darkness of trees, giant snowflakes falling in droves.

"Henry!" Susan cried, pleaded, her eyes shifting wildly from him to the road.

He relaxed his hands on the wheel, oddly mesmerized by the snow. Ding ding ding went the bells in his mind. He smiled absurdly.

Susan sat quietly, her eyes bugged. She guessed she was about to die.

A moment later the car seemed to be flying. It swerved off the road—Susan screamed—and it thudded to a stop in a shallow ditch. Instantly their hands flew to each other.

"Are you alright?" Henry said.

Susan burst into tears. They unbuckled their seat belts and hugged.

"Are you hurt?" he said.

"No," she gagged and brought her hands up to her face, making a bowl to shudder into.

Henry patted her with one hand and felt around for his phone with the other. Susan took her hands from her face and sat hiccuping for a while. Then she switched on the car light and stared at her husband.

Nervously, with shame, he stared back. Henry could see the fear fading in her eyes and the accusation rising. "What is *wrong* with you?" she said.

"Alright, save it. Let's just get out of this goddamn hole."

A few hours later they were in bed at the Holiday Inn, fully clothed, bickering, with rolled towels under their necks. They had been pulled out of the ditch by a huge, ham-colored man in a tow truck who demanded two hundred dollars in cash, which of course they didn't have on hand. So he drove them right to an ATM.

"It was like being *robbed*," Susan fumed.

"You're shouting," Henry said.

"You should've refused."

"We had no choice. That guy was clearly in cahoots with the cops. This is what they *do*."

"My *neck*," Susan moaned.

"You have whiplash. You're going to be fine."

"We should go to the hospital."

"So we can sit there for hours until some moron says we have *whiplash*? I won't do it."

"What if we hit our heads?"

"We didn't hit our heads," Henry said and sat up. "I'm turning off the light."

"Sometimes people hit their heads and they don't remember," Susan said, her eyes pleading.

"We didn't hit our goddamn heads. The windshield would've broken." He sighed. "I'm turning off the light."

"Leave one on," Susan said. "Please. This place gives me the creeps."

Henry said nothing. But he had to agree that the room was awful and somewhat like a cage, with its low ceiling and un-openable windows looking out onto the parking lot. Giant flakes of snow were still rushing through the air, quietly accumulating on the three cars in the lot. It looked so soft, Henry thought. The thing that almost killed them. He closed the slatted metallic shades and undressed, then walked back to the bed in his boxers and undershirt. Henry had pale, bony legs and the paunch of a genetically thin man who has overeaten for decades. "Let's get under the covers," he said to Susan but she said nothing, her mouth angrily pursed. He walked to the other side of the bed and peeled the tan blanket back, then climbed in despite Susan, who remained sternly in position, blinking at the ceiling.

When she finally did take off her clothes and get under the sheets, the same angry, fearful energy kept her eyes bugged. "I can't sleep," she said.

Henry muttered something, then slid right back out of consciousness.

"I keep thinking about the guy at the front desk," Susan said loudly. "Didn't he have kind of a *strange* reaction when we said we were in an accident? He looked like he thought it was funny."

"He *was* odd," Henry said, rousing with interest. "He looked a little like the guy that killed the dancer."

"What?"

"Remember the woman in the East Village who had the terrible roommate who killed her?"

"No," Susan said, as icily as she could manage.

"Was it the eighties?" He squinted. "She was a dancer, I remember that. And the guy cut her up and put her in a stew and fed it to the homeless in the park."

"God*damn*it, Henry."

"I remember reading about it in the *Voice*. It was this bald guy that did it."

Unable to move her neck, Susan went on staring, with great urgency, at the ceiling. "That's such a terrible thing to do to the homeless," she said.

Henry laughed. "It was a terrible thing to do to that little dancer!"

Susan's mouth squirmed as she animated the crime in her mind, eyes shining. "How did they find out?"

"I think there was a finger in the soup."

She groaned.

"And later on they found other parts of her in the apartment," Henry continued. "*Feet* perhaps," he said and Susan could hear the strange look of glee on his face. "And I think the homeless were blamed," he said. "As if they were somehow complicit by eating the soup."

Now engrossed in visualizing the stew, red-brown and bobbing with human meat, Susan had stopped blinking altogether. Henry still experienced her as a void. It actually relaxed him. "There are people who can be served anything," he said. "Because they'll *eat* anything."

Susan was quiet a second. "I would never come back from that," she said, a frost of revulsion in her eyes. "From eating someone I mean."

"Maybe you have," he said and yawned.

"Oh for God's *sake*."

"Well there's really no way of knowing," he said casually, sleepiness dulling his features once more. "And it's good that we don't know all the things we've consumed. It's the *knowing* that drives people nuts."

They were quiet for a while. Henry had his eyes closed. Susan stared brightly at the ceiling, her eyes drilling through it. "Henry," she said, "I don't think I'm going to be able to sleep." But he was already gone.

In the morning their necks hurt even more. Susan could barely sit up. After much complaining, they went downstairs and ate the complimentary scrambled eggs.

"Ugh. This was made in the microwave," Susan said, chewing. "I can tell."

They each drank two cups of the weak, tawny coffee, then put their coats on and walked out into the parking lot.

The roads had been plowed. The van looked *okay*, they agreed, brushing snow away, except for a deep scratch on one side. Susan ran her finger over it. "I'm driving," she said with a hostile glance and Henry said nothing. It was his way of agreeing.

They packed their things and drank more of the pale coffee, then bid farewell to the bald man at the front desk, who in daylight looked more pitiful than creepy. He seemed to be the only one working there.

On the way out of town they learned they were in La Porte, Indiana, a town that seemed to have embraced its own depression, with nothing but fast-food chains and car dealerships.

"It's so cheery and failed," Henry remarked.

Susan laughed. "What do you think people do here?" she asked.

"I don't know. Wait for their parents to die so they can buy a car?"

The following towns were much the same, one little museum of loss after another. "Americans are living badly," Susan said.

"And *proudly*," Henry smirked. "That's the problem."

He joked in the same sneering way all day, which relaxed Susan. But whenever it was quiet, her anxiety came lurching back, punching the landscape full of death traps. She drove slowly—too slowly—often holding her breath. And when the sun sank low in the sky, burning the horizon, it didn't matter how slowly she drove. Susan felt powerless the way people in movies were, people tied to railroad tracks, people with big luminous knives to their throats. *So many ways to die,* she thought, her eyes traveling to the wide gap of shadows beyond the road's edge. Susan pictured the two of them down there, dead or dying, the car on its side. "I'm a little bit afraid," she admitted.

"Do you want me to drive?"

"No," she replied. "That would be worse."

This silenced Henry. He leaned back in his chair with a glazed look of anger.

"We have to stop," she blurted.

"What?"

"I'm shaking."

"So let me drive!"

"*No.*"

She took the next exit and they went to McDonald's, where Henry sat gruntily consuming a burger in the crude white light.

Susan sipped her soda with averted eyes, eating the occasional fry. "We're such chickens," she said grimly.

Henry stopped chewing and stared. "What does that mean?"

"We've had our heads cut off," she said. "And we're running around."

"That's more activity than I see happening," Henry said curtly. Then he swallowed.

They checked into the Super 8 motel down the road. It was a square little room with dark purple carpeting and a jungle-print bedspread.

"I can smell every truck driver who ever showered here!" Susan hollered from the bathroom.

Henry was in bed, mindlessly thumbing through his notebook. Susan walked toward him with her brown button-down sweater hanging half off her body, the unclothed arm outstretched. She squatted next to the bed. "Feel this right here," she said, prodding her upper arm. "Is that a lump?"

"Hold on. I'm in the depths of a sentence," Henry said, jotting something down.

Susan waited with her arm out.

Finally Henry put his pen down and pressed the area gently. "I don't feel anything," he said.

She returned her exploring fingers to the arm. "I don't feel it now either."

Henry stared at her, at first with annoyance but then softly, with love. "I know you so well," he said.

"Maybe you do."

"Maybe?"

"I'm flirting with you."

"Oh," he said with a broad, intimate smile.

Susan changed into a long oatmeal-colored nightgown, then fetched a yellow legal pad from her bag. She crawled into bed and the two wrote in silence for a bit. Then she put her pen down and plunked her head onto his shoulder. "It's important to feel for lumps, you know," she said, peering down at his notebook.

"Yes," he said. "But don't *worry* so much."

"Why not?" Susan sat upright, staring. "Health is precarious." She waited for him to return her gaze. "There are so many little things that can ruin your perfect life."

Henry hummed.

Susan read his four-line poem. "I like it," she said, almost immediately. "I wrote one too." She handed him her pad. The poem was called "At Night" and featured a couple found dead in their car. The bodies were described with frank indifference, like they were apples. "It was written from the perspective of Satan," Susan explained. "That's why it's mundane," she said. "Because he doesn't care when people die."

"Well he likes it." Henry grinned.

"No." Susan shook her head. "He's indifferent. He hardly *notices*." She exhaled. "That's what evil is." Susan reached over and pointed to the third line. "How do you feel about that comma there?"

"I'd get rid of it. But I'm a pervert."

Susan laughed. "You get such a devilish smile on your face when you say something clever."

"I know. It's a smile I enjoy submitting to," Henry said, removing his glasses. He sank his head down onto the pillow with a great sigh.

"I'm not tired at all," Susan said.

"I am," Henry said. He looked at her a moment, eyes slivered. "Most of what we do together is sleep. Isn't that funny?"

"Hilarious."

"No, it's very intimate," he said seriously. "We enter our *dreams* together."

"Well," she said, "not really together."

"Right. We enter them privately. But our *bodies* are together. Think of movie theaters," he said, gripping her arm excitedly. "Isn't that funny? Movies imitate dreams and that's why we like them."

"You're right." Susan put her head on his shoulder and closed her eyes, knowing full well that she wouldn't sleep. She didn't even feel like trying.

Henry started to snore and she opened her eyes, then sat up with a small prick of terror. Snow was dashing by the window, heaping up on the sill. She looked down at Henry, who was sleeping in his usual way, like a frog on a slide in a laboratory. *"Look,"* she said loudly, giving him a shove.

"What?" he said, drunk with sleep.

"It's snowing."

"Go to sleep."

"We can't go on like this."

"What?"

"We can't drive the whole way there. I'm too afraid."

Henry sat up and turned on the light. "So what do you suggest we *do*?" he said nastily.

"A former student of mine lives in Minneapolis. Do you remember Amy?"

Henry only stared, his eyes flat with rage.

"I could get us as far as Minneapolis. I'm sure Amy will know someone who we can pay to drive the car."

"Who we can *pay*?" Henry raged. "So we can sit in the back like children?"

"No. We'll take a plane," she said cautiously.

"Oh *will* we?" he said with a scary smile. "So you've got it all planned out then?"

"I think it's best," Susan said, careful not to look at him.

Henry went quiet, his teeth clenched together. He hated Susan's grim authority, how it slowed everything down. She sat with her mouth drawn into a taut black line and looked eerily like one of the dominating nuns from his Catholic high school. *Sister Fish,* he thought, unable to remember her real name, only that it rhymed with fish. She was an awful, relentless woman with the speckled face of a trout.

He wished in that moment that he were a truly bad person, bad enough to desert his wife. To drive off on his own, speeding the whole way to Missoula. "You are un*believable*!" he shouted and Susan jerked, her green eyes bugged. It gave Henry pause. "I know you're scared," he continued with downcast eyes, plunging back into a softer fury. "But we'll get there, I promise. If you let me *drive*, for Christ's sake."

"It's not safe!" Susan burst into tears. "We don't even have snow tires." She shook her head. "I won't do it."

Henry said nothing, which was his way—despite insurmountable rage—of agreeing to her plan. "Good night," he said with unmasked contempt, then switched off the lamp. But for the first time in ages, Henry couldn't sleep. He groaned and sighed, writing speeches in his mind.

"Don't move so much!" Susan said.

"Pity I'm alive."

"Oh shut up."

"One day you'll wake up with a corpse."

"Shut up!"

"It's a horrible event I won't be present for," he laughed.

"I can't believe you."

"It's a *fact* that men die first."

"Shut up!"

"Fine," Henry grinned.

Susan stewed awhile, arms folded over her chest. "You write these *beautiful* poems," she said abruptly, twisting the word "beautiful" with scorn. "But you're a *sicko*. If people only knew . . ." She glared at the dark mound beside her, the stomach rising and falling with even breaths. He was asleep.

In the morning Susan groggily called Amy, who was delighted to hear from her, then aghast when Susan described the accident.

"I'm okay," Susan assured her, to Henry's disgust.

Amy said she probably knew someone who needed the money. And within the hour, she called back to confirm that a friend of hers—a guy named Luke—had agreed to drive the van.

Henry heard the words "five hundred dollars" spoken and

winced. But he remained dangerously quiet, mechanically packing his toiletries.

"Milwaukee," Susan called out a few minutes later.

"Milwaukee what?" Henry asked.

"I found two tickets from there to Missoula. It's a little out of our way . . . but cheap."

"Fine," Henry replied, zipping his bag.

In the car they were silent for over an hour, while Susan drove slowly, her face marked dimly with terror. The snow had melted but the weather application on her phone promised more. And after several coffees, her mouth had grown helplessly mobile, sealing itself tightly and then falling open, only to be bitten a second later.

Henry faced the side window, though he didn't register any of the drab shapes flitting past. He had sunk into one long poem and the words sounded off in his brain of their own accord. It wasn't pleasant. The words felt rancid inside him. Not a single one seemed worth writing down and besides, he didn't want to move his hand. If he reached for his pen, he thought he might make a fist and shatter the window instead.

By dusk Susan was exhausted. Her eyes traveled continually to the road's edge, where the concave earth looked bottomless, like one long hole leading to outer space. The steering wheel also seemed to have changed. It felt bigger in her hands, chubbier somehow. And it was breathing.

"I'm hungry," she said loudly, straining to keep her hands from flying off the wheel. She didn't actually feel the urge to eat but feared her starvation was awakening the snakes of her subconscious, giving them power.

She pulled into a gas station and wearily exited the car,

shaking out her hands as she walked to the bathroom: a concrete room of humming fluorescence with a urine-spattered
toilet seat.

Susan was spooked by her reflection in the mirror. She looked
positively gaunt, with a gray-green hue around her eyes. "God,"
she said aloud, staring at the wizened little face. *How could that be
me?* The more she stared, the more the white light seemed to penetrate her skin, spotlighting her skull. *I'm all bone,* she thought,
moving her face in the mirror until her flesh reappeared. It was a
relief but a minor one that teetered quickly back to self-hate.

"I look wrinkly and crazy," she declared upon reentering
the car, a packaged cherry Danish in hand. "Like a kind of veg-
etable that has no name."

Henry smiled with a sniff. They had apparently finessed
their fight down to a small war that now allowed for conversation, if only out of lonesomeness. And he was glad. "You're out
of your mind," he said. "But I love looking atcha."

Susan smiled weakly, with gratitude. It was a smile that could
have collapsed into a sob if she wasn't careful. She was so tired.

"Are you alright?" he asked, touching her arm.

"I don't know," she said. "I'm a little kittenish."

Henry smiled. "That's exactly what you are."

"There was a man by the register holding an umbrella,"
Susan said. "I thought it was a rifle."

"Oh honey." He touched her shoulder. "You're *exhausted.*"

Susan struggled to free the cherry Danish from its veil of
plastic. Henry watched a moment. Then he opened it for her.

She took a bite and wrinkled her nose. "This is disgusting,"
she said and continued to eat it. When the pastry was half gone,
she stuck it back in the plastic and set it down on her lap. "Eating
is a mistake," she declared. "I think starvation is the better choice."

"There are hospitals full of women who feel that way."

Susan laughed feebly. She watched as he finished the Danish.

Luke lived in St. Paul. They arranged to meet at his apartment, then he would drive them to the bus that would get them to the plane that would deliver them at long last to Missoula.

Henry frowned when Luke appeared at the door. He looked like a teenager, though as it turned out he was twenty-three. And handsome in a way that made Susan smile like a maniac. He had a jaw of dark stubble and soft-looking brown hair that he raked his fingers through compulsively. It occurred to Susan that he might have taken speed to cut through the harrowing boredom that lay ahead. She stared at him and realized that he reminded her a bit of Henry as a younger man.

She actually saw copies of Henry's younger self everywhere, always, glowing on street corners and in coffee shops. *He must see me too,* she thought. *All young and pretty, blooming from the body of some graduate student, some waitress.*

Henry rode up front with Luke, eyeing his driving while detailing the van's various quirks. The conversation quickly veered, by Luke's initiation, to the possibility of him crashing the car.

"I'm a really good driver," Luke said, now looking even younger than he had ten minutes before. "I'm sure everything'll go smoothly," he pledged. "But *say* I hit some ice or something. Will I be held responsible for—"

"No, no, *no,*" Susan chimed from the backseat, to Henry's horror. But he said nothing.

"If something happened to the car it would be our loss," Susan said.

"*Well,*" Henry interjected. "It would actually be my brother's loss. It's his car," he said with a steely glance in her direction.

"Regardless," Susan snapped. "We wouldn't hold you responsible."

"Well don't worry," Luke said, "I don't think anything like that's gonna happen."

"Of course not. You'll be absolutely *fine*," Susan cooed. "We would've been fine but we're just so *traumatized* by what happened."

"Totally." Luke nodded. "I get it." He touched his hair, blinking rapidly.

At the bus station Susan wrote him a check and he snatched it from her hand. It was stunning but somehow didn't feel rude, more a side effect of the manic energy that he so clearly contained. Susan was now certain he had rocketed himself into the night with a drug of *some* sort. His facial movements were quick, his pupils like a couple of bouncy little balls whapping around in a dark closet.

She read over his directions. "This all looks good," she said, patting his shoulder. "We'll see you there." They waved goodbye and Luke smiled like a demon in a school photo, then walked rapidly to the van.

The bus station was filthy and severe looking, with people of all ages huddled in groups, some sitting alone on their luggage.

"That guy was *on* something," Henry growled.

"We're better off, believe me," Susan said. "He won't fall asleep."

Henry didn't want to think about the hopped-up kid in his brother's van. It was too awful. And too *ridiculous*. He felt a little numb, looking around. "Waiting for a bus is like *being* the poor," he said.

"Come on. It's interesting."

"I can't sit with these people."

"You can and you will," Susan said sharply.

They parked their bags and sat on them.

"It's almost more depressing to see the ones with a little beauty," Henry mused, looking around.

"What ones?"

"That girl." He pointed. "The one in the purple coat."

"You think she's pretty?"

"I do."

"She's not that pretty."

"She's too pretty to be *here*. I wonder if she knows she has a choice." Henry sighed, staring at the girl, who had her head on the shoulder of a boy. "She could go to Manhattan," he said. "She could be a cocktail waitress."

"What a dream come true."

"Isn't that what pretty girls do while they're figuring things out?"

Susan laughed. "I suppose." Just then a tall man with a black backpack and round wire-rimmed glasses caught her eye. He stood near the wall, clearly alone. She forced herself to look away.

It was this same man who sat behind them on the bus, in the very last row, and promptly began talking to himself. The bus pulled away from the station and Susan stared up at the dark sky. The moon was yellow and half-hidden by clouds, peeking out like a sore eye.

At first unintelligible, the man's continued muttering soon grew loud and clear. "Don't you ever wanna blast someone?" he said and Susan stiffened. Then he went quiet, presumably to take in the response of his imagined comrade. Then he laughed.

Susan held her breath, listening as the man's speech slid back into muttered gibberish. She wondered how he had succeeded in

so many things. Like acquiring clothes that fit him and pre-
scription lenses. Or knowing the bus schedule and buying a
ticket. These were the sorts of simple tasks that she herself sometimes struggled with. She knew that if she ever went crazy, she
would function in *no* way. Her life would be over.

Henry seized her arm, startling her.

"Jesus!" she said.

"We have to move," he whispered.

So they carried their bags to the first free pair of seats,
which was more toward the middle of the bus.

"That was so scary," Susan said in a low voice.

"I know."

"I didn't think it was bothering you till you *grabbed* me. You
were so quiet."

"I was listening to him. I wanted to hear exactly what he
was saying." Henry blinked reflectively. "He said something
about a sword."

"He did?"

"That's when I grabbed you."

"God. It must be like a radio station in your head."

"Right." Henry sniffed. "I immediately thought of that guy
who murdered the kid on the bus."

Susan stared into Henry's face, dark with flashes of streetlight
rushing over it. "What guy who murdered the kid on the bus?"

"It was like two years ago. The guy decapitated this kid on
a Greyhound bus. You remember."

"No. I do *not* remember."

"Well I don't want to scare you."

"You're already scaring me!"

"Forget it."

They sat quietly a moment. Henry closed his eyes. Susan sat

up and looked nervously behind her chair. But it was too dark to see if the man was walking toward them with a sword. "Al-*right*," she whispered as she sat back down, irked by the curiosity Henry had planted. "So how did he cut off the head?"

Henry roused with a sniff. "What?"

"How did he cut off *the head*?" she repeated, a bit loudly.

"Oh. He had some sort of butcher knife I think. And he just attacked this very young kid out of nowhere. He said a voice in his head told him to."

"God."

"Everyone got off the bus and they locked the doors somehow with him in there." Henry rubbed his eyes. "And he just ran up and down the aisle carrying the head."

"Okay, *enough*."

"You asked."

Susan looked up at the yellow moon. She put her hand to her heart, feeling its speed.

At just past midnight they arrived in Milwaukee and took a cab to the airport. At a tiny table, Henry ate a dry turkey sandwich, sulkily examining it between bites. "I'm so starved for seasoning," he said.

"We're starved *period*," Susan said.

Henry stared at her. "Do you want some coffee?" he asked.

"No. More coffee might push me into another dimension."

Henry laughed. He finished the sandwich with one last, dissatisfied bite. Then they walked to the gate and sat in a couple of gray chairs. Susan put her head in Henry's lap. "I'm so weary," she croaked.

"I think you already told me that." Henry smiled.

"Oh shut up," she said and quickly fell asleep.

Henry watched a pair of young girls a few feet away. One had a head of short platinum curls, the other a long goldish braid. They sat cross-legged on the gray carpet facing each other, slouched over two separate piles of candy. They were trading. Their parents sat nearby, mutely pawing their phones. Henry wondered what sort of people gave their kids candy before boarding an evening plane. He watched as one girl, the one with the long braid, handed a Tootsie Roll to the other. She was compensated with a fat-headed lollipop. Fascinated, he watched a few more trades pass in the same girl's favor. Henry went from admiring her skills of manipulation to actually sort of feeling sorry for the one with the curls. *Maybe she's a little younger,* he thought, deciding she was being taken advantage of.

"Look," he said to Susan, patting her shoulder. "They're trading."

Susan opened her eyes only slightly.

"The one with the braid is hoarding all the good stuff," he said. "It's breaking my heart."

Susan's yawn curled up into a cat-like smile. "Cheapness is always expressed through candy at that age," she said and coughed, clearing the sleep from her voice. "It's the money of childhood."

Henry nodded, grinning. They watched as the girls ate from their two separate piles, then stumbled around in spacey states of bliss. "Kids are such drunks," Henry whispered.

"Staggering and gleeful," Susan added.

Soon they were called to board and Susan groaned. "Can I crawl?"

"Come on, love," he said.

And it was a surprising relief to enter the familiar capsule, to know that now nothing was expected of them. Even the lift-off was pleasant, easy to succumb to. They simply sat there, letting the rumbling machine have them, then the sky.

Susan looked down at the blinky orange-lit city. *How beautiful and monstrous,* she thought. She imagined the land below them two hundred years ago. Just dark and trees, a canoe riding by. "Look at it down there. It's so endless," she said to Henry. "Civilization. It only grows."

"Well, yes and no," he said. "There are things like blackouts that give you a little taste of what's possible. It's all so fragile really."

Susan nodded with a hum and leaned her head against his shoulder.

"I love the way you smell," he said and she smiled. It was the smile of someone who would never in her lifetime tire of flattery.

"And how is that?" she gleamed.

Henry gave her hair a deep, theatrical sniff. "Like bread," he said. "And the ocean."

To this she laughed. It felt good. "I love your mind," she said in an underwater way, nodding off on his shoulder.

"It kicks up a beautiful pearl once in a while," Henry said calmly, though his shoulder hurt like hell. "Susan," he said gently and kissed the top of her head. "Susan."

Memory

Alice is standing by the stove when she thinks of him. Joe. She lights the pilot, sets her red kettle down, and proceeds to stare into space. He had kissed her neck when she was fifteen. He had been old but she wasn't sure how old. He had graying hair and a red tan. Alice begins cracking her knuckles. She doesn't know what has summoned the memory of Joe's face and this bothers her. It is like a bat flung from darkness.

She can't remember how Joe knew her mother, only that his son had died, and that this gave him a lonesome, saintly quality. Her mom had been a single mom and so she needed help and he was glad to give it. He picked Alice up from school and sometimes took her out for sushi, which Alice liked. She remembers him sipping sake from a little white cup and talking about his son. She remembers him bringing out his wallet and showing her a bent picture of the boy, who wasn't a boy at all. Alice remembers being surprised to see a grown man grinning back from the snapshot. Alice had until that moment figured him to be a child.

Joe reported that his son had died during his freshman year in college and Alice watched the bubbles in her soda glass. She remembers that she wanted him to stop talking about his son. He was a little drunk and she felt herself recoiling from his grief, its endlessness. She remembers that he *did* stop talking about his son, almost as if he had heard her thoughts. He stopped talking altogether and stared at her and she could feel that he was admiring her.

"You're very beautiful," he said. Then, "Do you know that?"

Alice remembers how thrilled she was. She remembers that she could feel herself blushing, the heat rushing to her face. She remembers how this sublime feeling mingled almost immediately with dread. She remembers getting into Joe's silver car and putting the seat back slightly. This was something she always did but when she looked up at Joe, she wished she were upright. She remembers turning toward the purple sky, the sinking red sun.

"You have a tan on your belly," Joe said with a sideward glance. He was looking at the strip of flesh between her T-shirt and jeans.

"I know," she said.

Alice remembers that all the lights were off when she got home. She remembers mounting the stairs to her white house and going inside. She remembers sitting on the couch with Joe. She remembers him putting his arm around her, his gold wristwatch ticking in her ear. She remembers him moving her hair and kissing her neck. She remembers being amazed that a kiss could land so gently.

She remembers that she could not speak. If he had lunged toward her, she thinks now, she would have screamed. But it was as if he was moving underwater.

She remembers that he continued to plant soft kisses on

her neck and then her ear. She remembers that he asked her if she wanted to go to the bedroom. She remembers that her voice sounded strange when it arose, like it belonged to someone else. She said, "I have to do homework."

She remembers that he looked scared when she said this. She remembers him staring at her. It was as if she had in her hands a new and damning videotape of him. A tape she would have until she died. He continued staring and the tape's footage blazed between them. Then with a low smile, as if he were safe, he left.

Alice remembers going upstairs and getting into bed with all her clothes on. She remembers her sage green sheets and the round black clock by her bed, its loud, insistent ticking. She remembers picturing someone knocking from inside a coffin. "I'm not dead! I'm not!"

She remembers pulling a blanket over her head. She remembers hearing her mom come home. She remembers the phone ringing. She remembers her mom's laughter, how it seemed obscene. She knew it was Joe calling to see if her mom knew. And what *was* there to know?

She remembers breathing through her blanket. No words had yet glued themselves to the videotape in her mind. It only played itself again and again. She remembers that she was very still as she watched it. She remembers feeling like an animal with no language. She remembers that she closed her eyes but that she did not sleep.

Alice remembers going to school the next day. She remembers her depression, how adult it felt. She remembers wanting to tell her friends but feeling that there was nothing to tell. She remembers wanting to exaggerate certain elements of what had happened. She remembers wondering if what Joe had done was even a crime. She remembers wanting to say, "I was raped."

She remembers Joe picking her up from school in his silver car and how calm he looked, but with occasional flashes of worry, like dark fish darting under a frozen pond. She remembers how angry she was and letting it show. She remembers his worried smile. She remembers the car stopping in front of her house. She remembers saying, "I don't want to see you ever again."

She remembers him saying, "I'm sorry you feel that way." She remembers that his eyes were full of violence. She remembers sensing—almost smelling—that he wanted to kill her. Or that for a split second the thought was spreading itself in his mind. She remembers the terrible little theater of his eyes, which she had always thought to be blue. But looking at them in the afternoon glare, she saw that they weren't even a little bit blue. They were gray.

She remembers getting out of the car and running into her house and locking the door and locking all the windows. She remembers going into the broom closet and sitting in the dark until her mom got home. She remembers crawling out of the closet and telling her mom about the kisses. She remembers that her mom cried. She remembers looking away. She remembers their black cat, how he slunk through the flap door obliviously and hopped up the stairs.

She remembers her mom saying, "Did he do anything else?" and she remembers saying "No" and wishing that he had, if only to affirm that he was a bad man.

She remembers that her mom called Joe and left several messages. She remembers how they began as hysterical speeches and evolved to briefer, even-toned threats.

Alice remembers going to the police station with her mom in the morning. She remembers that there was one male cop and one female cop in a large room full of white light. She remembers describing what had happened. She remembers that they seemed disappointed. She remembers her mom asking what they were going to do.

She remembers the man saying, "We're gonna go to his house and talk to him." The woman said, "We're gonna give him a little scare."

Alice turns off the burner and stares at her red kettle. It has a dent on one side. She remembers her embarrassment at the police station and feels it anew. She wishes that Joe's kiss hadn't been soft. She wishes he had bitten her. She glances at her forty-two-year-old forearm, dark-haired and pale. Her gaze freezes there a moment. She wonders what she would do now if someone kissed her softly, someone whose kiss she didn't want. The police would laugh, she thinks. And maybe they had been laughing then. Maybe they hadn't been to Joe's house at all.

Alice pours herself a mug of tea and holds it with both hands, watching the steam rise and curl. She wonders if Joe has an Internet presence. She doesn't know his last name so there's no way of checking. *Maybe he's married,* she thinks. *Maybe he's with his wife right now and she's laughing at something he just said. Maybe they love each other more than they've ever loved anyone. Or maybe he lives alone but likes living alone. Or maybe he's dead.*

Teenage Hate

Joan and Dennis were lying in bed. It was late but the lamp on Joan's side was still on. She wouldn't turn it off. She had been talking about their daughter all evening.

"She said she hated me."

"They all say that."

"But do they really?"

"Yes."

"And it's not just me. Cindy hates *everything*."

"Teenagers are mean. They need to be. It's the first interpretation of seriousness."

Neither spoke for a few seconds.

"What is it?" Dennis asked.

"I'm just thinking about what you said. I think you might be right."

"Oh, I am."

In the morning Joan made pancakes and Dennis made coffee. Then they sat together sipping from their mugs. Under the table a cat careened into Joan's shin and slid away, purring wildly. They had two cats, one orange and one white, named Carrot and Sneaker respectively.

Cindy appeared in blue shorts and a white T-shirt. She was taller than both of her parents, with blonde hair and pale green eyes. Without a word she padded into the kitchen and withdrew a cereal box from the cupboard, then stuck half her arm in. After eating a few handfuls she walked off with the box.

"I made pancakes!" Joan called after her. Then she heard Cindy's door slam shut. "Now what the hell was that?" She turned to Dennis, her nostrils hard.

But he had barely looked up from his food. The sight of Cindy's new body made him cringe. There was something blurry about it, how she tipped moment by moment between woman and child. Cindy was so beautiful—almost too beautiful. And while Dennis looked away, the whole neighborhood was peeping. Now that she was fifteen it had only gotten worse. It seemed no glance in Cindy's direction did not attach itself to her as she moved grumpily through a room or down a hall or across a street. As a result she stayed home a lot, playing the same pop songs over and over until she hated them. It was summer and she had no desire to go to camp or spend time with any of her friends. Generally she looked tired because she was. Tired of marshaling the world's lust for her.

"I don't think she's eating enough," Joan said. "She lives on diet soda . . . these teenage girls—they're like automatons— they'll eat anything that does nothing." She caught his eye. "You think I'm controlling but I'm not."

He made a neat cut in his pancakes. "You can't conduct this conversation with yourself in front of me."

Joan had to laugh at that. She tucked a slice of butter under her top pancake and licked the excess off her knife. "I *had* to eat at the table when I was a kid. If I had behaved like her my mom would've smacked me so hard."

"Yes, well, my mother smacked me no matter how I behaved," he said. "We don't have to demonstrate the abuse we experienced."

Joan softened. "You're a lovely man," she said.

When Dennis went to work, Joan washed the dishes and cleaned the kitchen. Then she walked to Cindy's door and knocked.

"*What?*" came the voice of the demon on the other side.

Joan strode right in with a cheery show of confidence that made her daughter tense. Cindy distrusted her mother's smile. In fact the merriness of all middle-aged women felt fraudulent to her. They seemed dangerous with their tight grins and burning coal eyes. They were jealous of course and it made her lonely. It filled her with hate.

In her robe and slippers, Joan walked around freely. She picked a worn copy of *Franny and Zooey* off the bed and touched its fragile cover. "Are you reading this?" she asked.

"You can't just come in here." Cindy sat on the floor next to an open magazine.

"I loved to read when I was your age," Joan said. "But my brother was always stealing my books." She smiled reflectively. "He didn't even read them. He just put them on his shelf. What he wanted was my *enthusiasm*."

"Mom, get out."

"I believe this is *my* book."

"It was on the shelf."

"You can have it." Joan set the book back down on the bed. "It's good, isn't it?" she said, but there came no reply. Cindy sat with her arms crossed, a homicidal song in her eyes. Still Joan was too captivated to look away. It was a marvelous view of something utterly gone: her youth.

She left the room, leaving the door ajar. Then Cindy slammed it.

Joan walked to the bathroom and felt it too, the forbidden feeling: hate. Cindy had left the hair dryer on the floor and one by one the cats were examining it like a spaceship had landed. Joan shooed them away and the orange one jumped up onto the sink, then into the toilet with a splash.

"Carrot!" Joan cried.

The cat hopped out, shaking and appalled, then ran off.

Sighing, Joan wiped down the toilet seat and sat on it. Then a blast of music made her jerk, bracing the wall as she peed. It was a small apartment and the walls seemed porous, the way they spilled noise from one room into another. Many times she heard Cindy crying in there. Maybe, she thought, the shrill pop song was actually announcing such a moment.

Joan wiped herself roughly. She flew off the toilet, stomped to Cindy's door and stood there. Just then the song ended. But an instant later it began again, the canned screams. Joan's face tightened. Stepping away from the door, it occurred to her that she was a little bit afraid of her daughter.

It seemed there was only one thing to do so Joan did it—she left. She didn't know where she was going, only that she was going. Maybe she would never come back. Maybe she would jump in front of a car and a certain grim little girl would get a cold, hard taste of reality. But no, she would go on living. She knew it. She was doomed to function.

Joan walked out into the sun, past an ice-cream truck and a

pile of dog shit and an old man selling batteries. She walked on and on until she wasn't in their neighborhood anymore. She imagined herself getting thin this way, speed-walking through the streets for days, bolstered by hate.

A pair of wealthy-looking women walked by. They had such similar plastic surgery that they looked like sisters. It made Joan laugh. *Maybe I'm crazy*, she thought with the breeze in her hair. *But the world is deeply insane.* Suddenly she felt happier than she had in weeks. Joan looked up at the blue sky and thought it might be even more beautiful than her daughter.

She passed a man on a stool with his easel before him. He was painting a cheesy panoramic of some buildings, even though there was a drooling junkie behind him. *Why don't you paint that?* Joan wondered. A man bumped into her and she realized, as she had so many times, that she was invisible. It made her want to do something obscene like take her top off. But no, that would disgust people. She pictured herself getting arrested with her breasts out and felt incredibly sad. *There's no reward for being an older female,* she thought. *Because no one wants to look at your flesh.*

She didn't *feel* older, that was the confusing part. She felt seventeen, just as hungry. Maybe she always would. Maybe the energy that was sizzling and repressed in high school would keep unfurling all her life.

A cop on a horse clomped slowly by and Joan wiped the sweat from her upper lip. She wondered what it was like to be seized and made to carry people your whole life, then killed when you were old. She wondered if there were any wild horses left in the world. Joan felt herself slowing as she calculated the possible number of them—eighteen? Her feet hurt. She wiped her lip again, then tore her eyes from the doomed horse and hailed a cab.

———

At home it was quiet. The cats rubbed themselves against the backs of her legs, then walked about the kitchen meowing. "Calm down you lunatics," Joan said. She drank a glass of water. Then another.

Franny and Zooey lay on the table, facedown beside an open can of soda. Joan snatched the book up with a small flourish of anger. Opening it, the smell of aged paper jumped up into the air.

Inside was a loose photograph of herself as a teen, smiling in a pale pink romper, a yellow telephone beaming before her. Joan flipped the photograph over and read *1971* in blue ink. Abruptly she stuck the photo back in the book and walked with it to Cindy's door.

There was a round sticker by the doorknob. Maybe it had been there before but she couldn't be sure. It pictured a humanish cartoon rabbit giving the middle finger. Next to it there was a sticker that read WISH YOU WERE WEIRD in neon green letters. That one was old. Joan froze for a second, then knocked.

"Yeah?"

"Can I come in?"

"Do I really have a choice?"

"No." Joan opened the door.

"Why even ask if I don't have a choice?"

"Because I respect you."

Cindy let out a dismissive puff of air, making her doubt clear. She was lying on the bed, cell phone in hand.

"You left this in the kitchen," Joan said.

"On purpose," Cindy said.

"I gave it to you," Joan said. She seated herself on the bed and set the book down.

Cindy stared, her face a dark shield.

"I found this picture inside," Joan said and for a moment Cindy looked caught.

"It's me in 1971," Joan reported. She placed the photograph on the bed before her daughter, who hesitated, then picked it up.

"I saw it," Cindy admitted. Then, "I like how you looked. Everything was so pretty in the seventies."

Joan almost stopped breathing; she didn't want to break the delicate twig that suddenly held them together. "It *was* pretty," she said finally. "But if you were depressed it was really intense."

Cindy looked genuinely curious. "How?"

"Just gauzy and endless," Joan said. "It made me want to scream."

Cindy understood that. She laughed. "I like the yellow phone though."

"All girls wanted a princess phone in their bedroom," Joan said. "Mostly they were white and pink and lavender." She stared into space. "Actually, I don't know if they were ever lavender. But that would have been the perfect color."

Cindy had stopped looking at the photograph and Joan knew their time was almost up. She didn't want to sit and watch the sweetness recede—it was too excruciating. So with a small smile she stood and let herself out.

Later Dennis and Joan lay in bed reading. The cats sat at the window, staring out at something on the sill, their tails making question marks.

"Cindy saw a picture of me from 1971 today."

"Oh yeah?"

"She liked it." Joan rested her hands on her open book. "And the funny thing is that I remember how much I liked looking at pictures of *my* mom when she was younger."

"Because you didn't know her."

"That's exactly why." Joan lay there blinking.

"Look at them," Dennis said, pointing at Carrot and Sneaker. "I love a cat looking out a window." He paused. "It makes the window more beautiful."

"It's sort of monstrous though," Joan said. "That we don't allow them to partake in their own nature. Everything they want is out there," she said, gesturing toward the window. "But everything they have is in here."

They were quiet, watching the cats.

"The only justification is that we're keeping them alive," she added. "It's like we're God."

Dennis laughed. "But maybe it's not so bad," he said. "They never get what they think they want, so looking out the window is probably like watching TV."

"What a TV," Joan said. She thought of all the trapped creatures on earth, all of them watching the free world and waiting to join it. If there was no window to look through, there was the shimmering thought of one. There was a mind. They were all waiting because something better was out there for them on the other side. There had to be.

Orphans

Miranda found a seat toward the back of the room. A man left the coffee station and walked toward her, staring a moment. He had a very dirty face. *Homeless,* she thought and recoiled. Then he sat in the chair directly to her right.

The meeting began and her eyes swam nervously around the room, hunting for another seat. She spotted one but it was far away and she didn't want to draw attention to herself. She didn't want people to think *What a coward* or *What a stuck-up bitch.* So she remained in her seat, smelling the man.

She found it difficult to focus on the woman talking at the front of the room, hearing only stray details. She fidgeted, her eyes batting around. She felt so aware of how she might look in the chair: her scrawny body and big breasts, her stringy black hair. Everyone else seemed to be listening. *But that can't possibly be true,* she thought.

The woman said she often considered shooting herself in the head. This grabbed Miranda's attention. "I keep seeing my brains splattered all over the wall," the woman said and, audibly, the whole room's breathing changed. "I'm not drinking. I haven't drank in sixteen years. But the world still scares me." The woman grimaced, holding back tears. Then she started talking about the seventh step and Miranda's focus wavered. She could only focus when people detailed their sorrows. Otherwise AA had the empty feeling of a cult.

She glanced sideward at the homeless man, his filthy profile. He was older than her, with gunmetal gray hair and the deep, tanned wrinkles of a farmer. Her gaze lingered over the mystery of his features, each one shaded with dirt. Then he turned and grinned at her. It was startling. He had thin, darkly arched brows and very blue eyes.

Miranda smiled quickly and turned away, blushing profusely. She had the urge to bolt as she always did when any man showed even the slightest interest in her. But she only stirred in her seat, fumbling with her fingers in her lap.

After a half hour of keeping her eyes on her hands and the backs of other people's heads, the fizzy feeling of anxiety diffused. Miranda let her gaze drift back onto the man, wanting badly to confirm his continued interest in her. And there it was, beaming like a lit candle in a dark, dark room. He looked a bit like Jack Nicholson, she realized, with his boomerang eyebrows and wide cat grin.

It occurred to her that he could be high or drunk, but he didn't look it. Then she considered the possibility that he could be a thief. *And it would be easy to steal from me,* she thought, lacing her fingers together on her lap. But the truth was that she enjoyed the feel of his burning gaze, regardless of whatever sat lurking behind it. Who was he, this man who could stare and stare? He was filthy but handsome. *It's obvious,* Miranda thought. Anyone could see it. *Well not anyone,* she thought, commending herself for being able to take anything—and anyone—out of context. His context was just a lot of dirt and probably a very sad story. Miranda wondered what had ejected him into the wilderness of Manhattan. Then she imagined him emerging from the shower with a towel tied at his waist, clouds of steam gushing around him. She admired the look of him all clean in her mind: hair combed, nails scrubbed, his blue eyes electric against the pink of his cheeks.

But what if he's stupid? Miranda thought. This was not impossible. Often people radiated a smartness that simply wasn't there. And certainly this would be worse than him being high or drunk or a thief. She let the unhappy thought twirl in her mind a moment. Then she let it go. She was getting better and better at letting things go.

When the meeting was over everyone stood in a circle to pray aloud, holding hands. Miranda stalled a moment, clearing her throat, then took his grubby hand in hers. She said the prayer softly so as to hear his voice. "God, grant me the serenity to accept the things I cannot change," came a high, funny voice. "Courage to change the things I can. And wisdom to know the difference."

When their hands parted they looked at each other. She had a crush. It was shocking. She cleared her throat. The room had grown loud like a cafeteria, everyone chatting and collapsing their chairs.

"Hello," she ventured.

"Hi," he said.

"I'm Miranda," she said, hating the sound of her name, how desperate it seemed to sound in any context.

"Drew," he said with a nod.

In a soft voice, feeling embarrassed, she said, "Do you have anywhere to go?"

He paused. "There's a place."

Miranda nodded, admiring his vagueness. There was a certain dignity about it. "Do you want to go for a walk?" she asked.

Again he paused. Then, without answering, Drew gathered his things: a backpack and a smaller bag with handles, both blackened with filth. He followed her as she left the building and in the streetlight they walked alongside each other in silence.

It was late August. A cool breeze stroked them from six different directions, reassembling their hair.

"Are you a Christian?" Drew asked.

"No," Miranda said, laughing a little.

"So what's your story?" he asked, which made her nervous.

"Well I've been sober for a couple years but I just started going to meetings. I mean . . . I haven't spoken yet."

"Why not?"

"I guess I don't know what I'd say."

"You don't have to know." He paused, walking a little slower. "I mean, you *do* know."

"I do?"

"Yeah, I think . . ." He scratched his jaw. "I think the thing in your mind is the thing to say."

Miranda was quiet. Then she said, "I like that." It was so easy to imagine him clean because, in a way, he already was. His mind was. And the fact of his filth relaxed her. She wasn't worried about her clogged pores or the murky scent of her underarms. She felt very civilized, almost queenly. The dreamy feeling mounted until she was drunk with it. "Do you want to come over?"

He looked stricken when she said this. They had stopped walking. The stiff look of caution first softened around his mouth. It took a moment. Then the old grin grew in its place.

Miranda said nothing. She only faced him with the wide,

emotional eyes of a silent film star. She hoped he didn't think she was whorish. Because she wasn't. She thought about sex constantly but she hadn't had any in a while.

"Alright," he said. *"Okay."* He was smiling widely now. "Are you sure?"

"Yeah." But she wasn't sure. She pin-balled between arousal and revulsion, which fascinated her. It made the two sensations seem like old friends, sizzling together in one pool of wanting. *Yes,* she thought to herself as they mounted the stairs of her apartment. *No* when they walked into her living room. *No* again when he set his bags down on the floor. Then *Yes* when she made him a sandwich and he ate it. *Yes* when he said her apartment was nice. *Yes!*

It wasn't a nice apartment. He was being kind and it felt good. Her last boyfriend had called her apartment a dump. The day they broke up he looked around and said, "Fucking dump."

"Can I use your shower?" Drew asked.

"Of *course.*" She fetched him a yellow towel and he disappeared into the bathroom, shutting the door.

He was in there for a long time. Miranda unhooked her bra and yanked it out from under her shirt. She smoked three cigarettes in a row, then cleared the candy wrappers from the windowsill by her bed.

Finally the door opened a crack, his face peeking through. "Is there something I can wear?" Steam poured from the door.

"Oh. Sure." She looked around, stumped, then settled on her silk robe, beige with navy polka dots. He took it uneasily, which made her laugh.

Drew walked out looking very uncomfortable and sat on the couch. Miranda joined him and smiled sleepily. She liked being sleepy, how it felt vaguely beer induced. "How do you feel?" she asked.

"I feel good," he said, nodding. "I don't know about the robe though."

Miranda laughed. Drew looked nervous and that relaxed her. She felt almost predatory. "You look great," she said. "I mean you looked great *before* but now I can really see you." Without hesitation, Miranda took his wet head in her hands and kissed him. It was a forceful, passionate kiss. Her hand swam over his thighs and then between them, where it froze and was retracted.

A horrible, breathless silence fell over them.

"I couldn't tell if you knew," Drew said.

"I didn't," Miranda said, stunned. "Of course I *didn't*."

"Are you mad?"

"No." Miranda shook her head. "That's not it exactly. I just . . ." She got up and walked to the other side of the room, her arms folded. "I've never kissed a woman."

They stared at each other. A disturbed expression was quietly building on Drew's face. "I'm transgender."

"I feel fucked up," Miranda said. "Like I'm *seeing* things!" She walked back over to the couch and sat down, staring at Drew with open horror. "You look so much like a man," she said.

"I know that," Drew said. His pained expression was now morphing to one of pure anger. He marched to the bathroom and shut the door.

In seconds he emerged in the same dark rags, zipping up his fly.

"What are you doing?" Miranda demanded, but Drew said nothing, crossing the room and bending for his bags. "Don't go," Miranda pleaded in a new voice, a child's voice, grabbing Drew by the arm. She hated when people left. She hated when *anyone* left.

Drew turned his head and stared.

"*Please,*" Miranda said. She was crying. "Will you please just sit down."

Drew said nothing. After a moment he sat on the couch and sighed.

"Do you wanna lie down with me?" Miranda asked, wiping the tears from her eyes.

"What the fuck?" Drew looked appalled. But still he followed Miranda to her bed and they lay down staring at each other, the tangy stink of Drew's clothes filling the air between their faces. Strangely Miranda liked it.

Hours later they were both naked under a scratchy blue blanket, passing a cigarette back and forth between them, a soft breeze pushing through the window.

"Did you always know you were a man?" Miranda asked. "I mean when you were younger."

"Well." Drew took a long, reflective drag. "I knew I was different but I didn't know exactly what to call it—I just knew that I hated my name."

"What was your name?"

"Gloria."

"*No.*"

"Yes." Drew shook his head. "So wrong, right?"

Miranda nodded. "You are the *furthest* thing from a Gloria."

"Thank you," Drew smiled. He handed Miranda the cigarette and she took a long suck.

"So I renamed myself," Drew said. "At age six."

"You named yourself Drew?"

"Drew came later. As a child I was Daniel."

Miranda stared. "Your parents allowed that?"

"I had a single mother. She was very encouraging."

"That's incredible," Miranda said. "This was the fifties, right?"

"Yeah."

Miranda wanted to ask so many questions. She was smoking like a fiend.

"Look at you," Drew laughed.

"I know." Miranda smiled, handing the cigarette back.

"A name is all fantasy, you know?" Drew puffed thoughtfully, then flicked the cigarette out the window. "Why should anyone control that fantasy but you?"

Miranda smiled. She thought of other names besides Miranda. *Allison, Jennifer, Betty, Veronic—*

"I remember when I took baths as a kid I would stare at myself in the faucet—it made my nose look big—which I liked. I looked more like a man." Drew scratched his jaw, staring into darkness. "Man isn't really the word—but I looked more like myself."

Miranda nodded, though she didn't understand.

"I don't believe in gender as a binary *regime*—two categories with the whole human race crammed in. But it's a lot less disturbing for me to be called sir than *ma'am*," he said, warping the word *ma'am* with contempt. "So that's how I live."

"As sir."

Drew smiled. "Yeah, except no one actually calls me sir. They say man or mister. Or they say nothing." He paused. "Part of being trans is that language fails you." He ran his fingers through his hair. "All I ever wanted was to be seen as the person I am. And that person isn't male or female."

Miranda smiled. She had never been so turned on in her entire life. She sat up and lit another cigarette, then leaned against the wall taking long drags, her face obscured by darkness.

"What is it you do," Drew asked, "for money?"

"I wait tables. But really I'm a writer," Miranda said.

"Seriously?"

Miranda nodded. "What's that look for?"

"Nothing. I just—I didn't know I was hanging out with a camera."

They both laughed. Then Miranda started coughing.

"Jesus. How much do you smoke?" Drew asked.

"A lot."

"It's funny that you smoke lights," he said. "I mean there's no point. You suck em so hard."

"I know," Miranda said with shame, stubbing the cigarette out on the window ledge. "I've *tried* to stop. But time passes incredibly slowly without cigarettes. A day goes on for *weeks*." She began fondling her hair. "I can't deal with that kind of time."

Drew smiled. He reached up and felt around for Miranda's breast. "Your *heart*," he said.

"What?"

"It's about ready to pop out of your chest."

"Stop it. You're *scaring* me."

"Sorry. I'm really protective with people. With everyone but myself, that is."

A car alarm began wailing in the distance and Miranda shut the window. Drew stared at her. His face was lit now by moonlight. "Have you published anything?" he asked.

Miranda shook her head. She was a little devastated by the question. "No. I do *try* though," she said. "Whenever I write a good story, I try to find a home for it." She sighed. "But it always winds up an orphan. Then I write something else."

"That would be a good book title though. *Orphans*," Drew said.

"It *would*." Miranda switched on the gooseneck lamp by the

bed and wrote ORPHANS on a yellow Post-it. "Do you mind if I use that?"

"Not at all."

"If I wrote a story about you—I mean—about *us*, that's what I'd call it."

Drew seemed to like this idea. "How would you describe me?"

"I don't know. I would say you kind of changed reality for me."

Drew tipped his head. "Explain."

"Well you make it seem like everyone has their own gender."

"That's good," Drew said, his eyes marked with pleasure. "Because everyone does."

A Coffin

He is sitting at the kitchen table, staring hard at it. His mother just called and he's replaying the conversation in his mind. She said, "Shirley's dead." Shirley is his sister. Was. And talking to his mother was not like talking to an actual person. It was like turning on the radio for a minute. Because she makes herself a stranger. She speaks in a flat and even way, like she was raised by machines. And he is not surprised that she is this same demented ghost on the day of her daughter's death. He is even a little comforted because he's a demented ghost too.

So this is my reaction, he thinks. *I feel nothing.* It occurs to him that he is very dirty. He's been wearing the same shirt and underwear for two days. He was dirty before he got the call so it's no excuse. And the thought of showering or even changing his underwear feels impossible, like he would upset the delicate ecosystem under his clothes.

What surprises him is that he is not surprised. *Shirley even sounds like the name of a dead person,* he thinks. He almost laughs.

She had been in medical school and dropped out. She

decided to become an interior decorator and then decided not to. She liked to sing but she could only sing drunk. *Ambivalence is a low life-force,* he thinks. *She didn't even like being drunk.* He remembers her crawling over to him at a Christmas party and saying, "I need help." She was laughing though, which disturbed him. "Stop laughing," he said, taking her by the arm.

Then he realized she was crying and his face closed up. "Stop it," he said and his recoiling only made her cry harder. He remembers her splotchy face before she threw it down onto his lap. He feels her particular weight and his eyes fill with anger, then awe. *She will never cry again,* he thinks.

He leaves the kitchen and sits in a big navy cushioned chair. The television is on and it looks like a crime drama is playing. There are two faces having a serious conversation. The actors make small ugly expressions the way normal people do in pain and it seems a little obscene, like they're making fun of tragedy. He turns it off.

He wonders when he will die in relation to all his friends. *Will I be the last one standing? Or is Shirley prelude to the surprising event of my death* next week? He imagines a group of people discussing the strangeness of their concurrent deaths over coffee.

He calls the woman he's dating and she comes over. He regrets having called her. Not because he dislikes her. Because he has now realized that he wants to be alone.

She guides him to his bed and they sit down. He doesn't want to have sex. He makes that very clear. Then he announces that Shirley thought she had been a cat in a past life. "Because she *loved* cats," he says. "I couldn't be nice to her when she said stuff like that."

The woman smiles patiently. When it has been quiet awhile,

she says, "I had a friend who thought he was a passenger on the *Titanic*."

"What an idiot," he says instantly.

She stares at him.

"That's like saying I was a pharaoh in Egypt," he says.

She laughs.

"What a mundane mind," he says.

"He wasn't an idiot," she smiles. "He just thought he knew what people wanted to hear." She looks into her lap. "And the truth is that a lot of people *do* like hearing that sort of thing."

"What people?"

"Ordinary people."

He nods. She rubs his leg and stares into his eyes. He doesn't like it. He moves his gaze to a gray corner of the room.

"She was so miserable," he declares. "All the fucking time. I think she wanted to be really successful or famous or something. But she couldn't even hold a job."

"That's the thing about being young," she says. "You have something the world wants but the world doesn't know it yet."

This gets his attention. "I don't know if Shirley had anything the world wanted." He sighs. "She kept changing her mind. It's like she died of vagueness."

They lie down in their clothes and she holds him tightly. He feels restless and like an alien. He feels that he misses someone. He thinks it must be someone he used to date and wonders who. But he realizes that it is no single person. Because he has felt this brand of alien his whole life. *Each new relationship frames it a little differently,* he thinks.

Then he thinks back on his mother's voice over the phone. What she said at the end of their conversation was "She should be in a coffin." Then, "Your father wants an urn." He feels disgusted. He thinks it sounds like his parents are debating how to serve his sister to the family, how to roast and season her body. And all for the occasion of their grief, which is more an embarrassed sense of duty.

The truth is that he's hearing things. The room is quiet but there are several voices competing in the sewer of his thoughts.

He can't tell if it's Shirley or a woman he dated or one he's never met but a woman in his head is screaming and there's a laugh in her voice. *Maybe someone's chasing her, trying to tickle her,* he thinks.

He also hears what some gum on the street might hear during a storm, shoes and a million raindrops coming down like spankings.

Then he hears a dog alone. A dog in a car, barking its heart out.

The Hitch

Dawn woke up with a fever. It had snowed and the window poured with brutal white light. She pulled the blanket up over her shoulders, squinted in agony, then struggled into her slippers and shuffled to the kitchen.

Laurel sat reading the paper, sipping coffee from a Smurf mug. She wore what she always wore, a 1960s school uniform, gray stockings, and black penny loafers. It solved the problem of what to wear, she said. "Because this is always the right thing to wear." Laurel had big dark eyes and a giant head. Her body was quite small by comparison and from far away the disparity made her look like a child. But up close, she looked every bit of her twenty-five years and even older. Laurel's face was shadowy and broken down from years of chain-smoking and binge drinking. When men walking behind her shouted lewd things on the street, they were alarmed at who they saw when she turned her head. Laurel joked about it. She said it was a gift, her weather-beaten face. She said: "The world is a scary place for little girls."

"I think I have a fever," Dawn said, clutching her skull with both hands.

"So stay home," Laurel said, not looking up from her paper.

"I can't."

"Why?"

"I just can't."

Laurel looked up, irritated. "You're not an animal."

"What does that mean?"

"If you were an animal you'd have to push the cart no matter how you felt."

"But I *am* an animal. I have to push the cart."

Laurel glared.

"I can't lose the money."

"I'll *lend* you the money."

Dawn stared into space. "Fine," she said and walked back to her room. But once she heard Laurel leave, she got back out of bed and took two aspirin, then dressed and went to work.

Outside she watched the white of her breath. She passed a bum in a Santa hat, then a determined-looking blonde with a shopping bag. Just past eleven a.m., the Lower East Side was already crawling with shoppers of a particular sort. People with money. Dawn walked stiffly, peering at them. She had grown up in the neighborhood and felt increasingly like an outsider. Her rent-stabilized apartment was one of a remaining few and she joked that it was her inheritance, a shaky one. Her mother had left it to her when she moved to Los Angeles and Laurel had lived there with her ever since.

Dawn worked at a gift shop just blocks from the apartment. The awning was pink and dirty. It read SMALL WONDERS in two-foot black letters. The store was kitschy and cramped, shelves packed with a rainbow of plastic miniatures and gag gifts: eight balls,

Kewpie dolls, and Jesus bobble heads, along with depressingly retro East Village–themed goods like CBGB T-shirts and mugs made to look like the iconic Happy to Serve You coffee cups of the nineties. It made Dawn grimace to sell these fragments of her past. After a few snide comments, she had been stationed permanently at the back of the store, behind a long glass case featuring the higher-end goods: watches, jewelry, and cuff links, mostly.

The other girl who worked there didn't say anything when Dawn came through the door, nor did she look in Dawn's direction. She was tall and somewhat beautiful the way still and quiet people can be. Her name was Sylvia and her quietness was a radiant sort, one flaming with anger. Dawn forgot she was there for long stretches of time. Then suddenly Sylvia would speak.

"You have a really bad memory," she said when Dawn couldn't remember the price of a ceramic gnome. Sylvia stood with her arms crossed, watching Dawn's face squirm.

Sylvia was right. Dawn couldn't retain any of the prices. Nor could she answer anyone's questions about the merchandise. Did the watches have warranties? Were *all* the clocks made in China? She had no idea.

But Dawn didn't believe she had a bad memory. Not really. She just had a way of protecting her mind from all the boring details of daily life. If something didn't leave a blazing impression, it was immediately ejected from her cruising brain.

Her curiosity was reserved for more captivating subjects, like all the customers in their hats and gloves, shuffling around in a grabby trance. She loved watching them. She loved that it was part of her job, monitoring everyone to see if they needed help or if they were stealing. It seemed there was no other place where this sort of staring was acceptable.

Christmas was a few weeks away but still the customers

dawdled, browsing to no end. "It's like a petting zoo for capitalism," Dawn smirked. But Sylvia only glared in return, her arms tightly crossed. Dawn's smile faded. She was parked in her usual spot behind the glass case and the aspirin was wearing off. She stood perspiring under the hot white lights, her hair getting shiny and limp.

Dawn was supposed to meet her father that night for dinner and she kept picturing herself at the restaurant, the horrible silence pounding between them. She pictured herself saying: "I want to meet my family." She repeated the words in her mind several times, until they felt like a prayer. She had wanted to meet her father's side of the family since she was a child but he had always refused her in a vague sort of way, saying he would think about it or just staring for a long time before changing the subject. She was sure his family didn't know she existed. It seemed no one knew. At his sixtieth birthday party, Dawn had shocked an entire roomful of his friends. "I had no idea he had a daughter," they all exclaimed, which in retrospect seemed rude. *They should've lied,* Dawn thought.

She looked around the room and tried to guess which customers were fathers. Then, as if summoned by her thinking, one approached her. He brought his open wallet onto the glass counter and took out a small photo of a very pretty brunette, then handed it to her. "That's my daughter," he said while staring blankly at the jewelry, like a dog looking at a television. "What do you think she would like?"

"She's very pretty," Dawn said, lingering too long with the little face.

"I know," he said, smiling quickly.

Dawn recommended a pair of pearl studs and he stared at them. She held one pearl up to her earlobe.

"Okay," he said and Dawn was very moved. She almost cried. *He could be a bad man,* she consoled herself. But he didn't look like a bad man.

Dawn brought the earrings to the register, where Sylvia placed them in a white box and looped a glossy red ribbon around it, tying a tight bow on top.

Dawn watched the tidy spectacle in a slouching daze. When the man left, Sylvia turned with a cutting stare. "What's with you?" she said. "Are you *high*?"

"*No.* I was just . . ." Dawn broke off. Her face had drained of all color. "I was just thinking."

"Well don't." Sylvia walked past her. "Anyone could steal from you right now."

Dawn walked home weepy and disoriented, her fever breaking. When she got in the door, Laurel was sitting at the kitchen table drinking whiskey from a Batman mug. The big bottle of brown booze sat before her, uncapped and half gone. Beside it sat a fish-shaped ashtray, loaded to capacity with short and long butts. "I can't believe you went," she said, her enormous head swiveling in Dawn's direction. Laurel still had her uniform on but she'd peeled her stockings off. They hung from the back of her chair.

"I've only been there a week. I can't just call in sick." Dawn sat down and sighed. "Sylvia hates me."

"Who?"

"The other girl who works there."

"Oh. So what."

"She asked if I had a drug problem."

"Well you do," Laurel smirked. "But the drug is *you*."

"It's true! I still can't wrap gifts . . . I'm not even allowed."

"So what."

"Stop saying that."

"You wanna be one of those strange high-octane charm machines? People who *fold* things really well?" Laurel sneered. "They're nuts and stupid."

"But I should at least be able to—"

"There are no intellectual slackers," Laurel declared. "These people . . . they have no curiosity. You belong in the eighties." She took a long drink from her mug. "You know Jim Jarmusch sold popcorn at St. Marks Theatre. He was this freaky white-haired guy. He had a pompadour."

"How do you know this stuff?"

"My mother told me."

Dawn pictured the eighties in lower Manhattan, lush with possibility. It depressed her. "I don't get why artists still move here," she said.

"Be*cause*," Laurel said, "they wanna drink with other smart, disappointed people." She raised her mug. "Want?"

"I'm sick."

"It's good for that."

"No. I'm meeting my dad in like an hour."

Laurel stared coolly, then looked away.

Dawn watched her, knowing full well that refusing a drink was tantamount to betrayal in Laurel's mind.

"I thought you hated him," Laurel said.

"I still do. I can't believe my mom slept with him."

"They're back together?"

"No. I mean that she *ever* slept with him." Dawn tried to picture her dad as a cute younger guy. It actually wasn't that hard. "My aunt told me my mom tricked him into impregnating her. Like, they had broken up and she went to this bar where she knew he would be."

Laurel poured more whiskey into the Batman mug and set it before Dawn. "You can't trick someone into fucking you," she said.

"That's what I think. It was *his* choice. But I guess he figured that if she got pregnant, she'd get rid of it." Dawn hesitated, then sipped from the mug and grimaced.

Laurel smiled. "So you're the trick," she said. "That makes sense."

"The what?"

"*I'm* the mistake," Laurel said. "My parents didn't mean to have me." She grinned, proud somehow. "And my brother was the gift. Because my mom didn't really want kids but my dad did. She wanted to give him that." Laurel smiled again. "So you're the trick."

Dawn nodded. "I guess I am."

"You always say your dad wishes you'd never been born. So that's why. He didn't have a say."

"Well neither did I."

"Oh stop," Laurel said kindly. "Thank *God* your mom tricked him. I mean, thank *God* he was at that bar."

"I don't know why we have to bring God into it."

"Forget God. I'm just really glad your parents fucked that night."

"Well thanks," Dawn laughed.

But Laurel seemed not to hear her. She was staring just past Dawn's ear at nothing in particular, her eyes wide. "It's weird that some precise sexual act produced us," she said.

"Yeah. It's like the porn you can't have."

This excited Laurel. "But what if you *could*?"

Dawn stared at her, waiting for the speech she could feel burning in Laurel's thoughts. Her enthusiasm was always this way, like a fire that begins in the basement and quickly climbs throughout the house, radiant and snarling. "I mean, what if you could *see* that sex?" Laurel said, obsessed. She was very erect in her chair now. "I mean what if you had that technology?"

"What technology?"

"It would be like a solution," Laurel said carefully. "Made from a plant discovered in Brazil or somewhere." She paused, piecing the trembling bits of her fantasy together. "And when you applied it to your skin, it would reveal that your cells were taking pictures all the time. So your skin had a memory of its whole long photo shoot. Even of events that *predated* the body."

Dawn smiled. She looked down at the empty mug in her hands and refilled it, almost to the brim. "And how would they discover that the plant did all this?" she asked, smiling.

"Well because everyone who came into contact with it— like whole villages—were having these strange dreams. And it was always the *same* dream." Laurel had a sleazy grin now. "The scene of their conception."

"You're such a fucking pervert."

"And once they created the solution it would become like a business. People would *pay* to see the sex that spawned them. All porn would become this . . . specific past," Laurel said slowly. "And eventually it would even take the place of having sex." She lit a cigarette giddily and expelled a cloud of smoke. "It would be called Pornogenesis," she said with satisfaction. "Everyone would go to these little booths that were actually kind of like spas. And afterward they would sit out front in robes and share about their Pornogenesis. The slang term would be 'the hitch.' People would be like, so how was your hitch?"

"You have the face of a fanatic, you know that."

"I do know that." Laurel took a long smug drag, reacquainting herself with the exquisite distance just past Dawn's ear. "And people could also see each *other's* hitch," she said, tapping a long column of ashes into the crowded ashtray. "You could see the sex that spawned celebrities. Even Hitler. They'd figure out how. And eventually you'd pay to get yours blocked."

Dawn glanced at her phone. "Shit," she said. "I have to go."

"Oh come *on*," Laurel whined, clearly hurt to be abandoned mid-epiphany.

"I'll be late!"

"You're always hurrying somewhere awful."

"I completely agree."

"Are you really gonna go share a *meal* with that fucker?"

"I have to talk to him."

"About what?"

"You know."

Laurel nodded. A long plume of smoke exited her mouth. "What exactly did he say the last time you asked to meet them?"

"He's never given me a straight answer. Once he said he'd think about it." Dawn drained the Batman mug. "He obviously doesn't want me to meet them."

Laurel nodded. "Okay. Just . . ." She stubbed her cigarette out, wedging it in with all the rest. "Just don't be too *nice* to him." She fingered a fresh cigarette from her pack. "You're too goddamn nice."

Dawn's dad sat at a square wood table in a sushi restaurant, the light of a white paper lantern cast over him. His smile was purely muscular as he waved to her. It lacked the radiant tones of love. Not because he didn't love her, Dawn decided as she walked toward him. But because his love lived somewhere underground, like a deformed animal raised in pitch darkness—tortured. *What was done to you?* she wondered.

"Hello," he said.

"Hi," she said, unwinding her nubby black scarf. Her eyes were glassy, her cheeks and nose very pink. Panting slightly, she hung her coat over the back of the chair and sat down.

Dawn had enjoyed being drunk on the walk over, but now, sitting across from her father, she had to strain to keep his face from swirling. "How are you?" she asked, mopping her neck with her sleeve.

"My feet are killing me," he said. "I have bruises on my soles. They won't heal cause I can't afford to take off work." He eyed her response and she was careful not to give one.

"For them to heal I can't be standing all fucking day," he clarified.

"That's horrible," she said flatly. Her father always opened with an illustration of his poverty. It was to Dawn's mind a method of discouraging any requests for money, which angered her. She wondered if his feet really hurt and decided that they probably did. But the story still stank of cowardice. "My feet hurt all the time," she said after a moment of silence. "I wonder if I get that from you."

This suggestion of their totemic connectedness seemed to alarm him. "I don't think so," he commented. "They never hurt when I was younger."

"My feet *kill*. I have a new job. I'm standing all day," she said.

"Well I'm sorry."

The waitress appeared and they each ordered without having looked at the menu. He ordered only an Asahi beer. She ordered three different sushi rolls, suddenly ravenous and desperate to sponge up some of the circulating booze in her gut.

They exchanged more information about the parts of their bodies that hurt. His upper back, her lower back. His knee, her molar. By the end of the list they both sat blazing with self-pity.

Using her fingers, Dawn smeared wasabi over her tuna roll, then squeezed lemon over it. She loaded one into her mouth and swallowed after only a few chews. "I'm still working on the collection of stories," she said, knowing full well he wouldn't have asked. "It's coming along really well."

"That's good," he said absently, staring past her shoulder at a woman coming through the door. "Have you read *Moby-Dick*?"

"No. You've asked me before and I said the same—"

"Talk about a good book," he said. "*That's* what you should be reading."

She looked at his nose. There was a tiny black hair sprouting from the tip of it. "I want to meet your family," she said.

For an instant he looked frightened and it made him look younger. Then he turned back to stone.

"I can't believe I'm saying this again. I mean . . . I'm *embarrassed*." She looked down at her food. "And I don't want to *hate* you." She fixed her eyes on him and they stared at each other for what felt like minutes.

"I'm really not in touch with any of my brothers," he said finally, severing eye contact. "I wouldn't even know how to call them."

"That isn't true . . ." She folded her arms and began shaking her head. "You're lying to me!"

Everyone in the restaurant turned and stared.

"Calm down," he whispered sharply, nervously, like a criminal.

Dawn didn't calm down but she fell silent. She stood up and put her coat on.

"What are you doing?" He looked astonished. "Hey, now hold on."

The moon was low and yellow and Dawn walked without looking back, salt crunching under her boots. She ran through a red light and a taxi almost killed her. The driver stopped the car and yelled "Moron!" but Dawn kept running. She passed snowy rows of roped-up Christmas trees, wreathes with gold bells and fat red ribbons and Santa heads glued on. The woman selling trees appeared suddenly in her black hat and Dawn leapt away with a scream. She skidded on some ice, toppling forward onto her hands and knees. The fall was so shocking that she remained dog-like for a long moment before raising herself up.

"Are you alright?" the woman in the black hat asked.

Dawn didn't dare look at her. "I'm fine," she said, almost meanly, sinking her injured hands into her pockets. She walked off with tears in her eyes, burping up fish and whiskey all the way home.

Laurel was on the sofa reading, a blue granny-square blanket over her legs. She threw it off the instant Dawn appeared. "What happened?"

"I really don't want to talk about it."

"Oh he's a *fool*," Laurel said, dashing over. "The only thing he got right was you." She held Dawn tightly. "And he doesn't know it. He can't *bear* to know it."

"I'm just tired of caring," Dawn croaked. "I mean why do I *care* so much? Is this the human condition?"

"For some people." Laurel grinned. "And then there are the people who just kill people. They care about other things."

Dawn laughed a little. "I have to lie down," she said, resuming her pained, vacuous expression.

"Okay." Laurel hesitated. "Do you wanna sleep in my room?"

"No. I'll be fine."

Dawn forced herself to drink a full glass of water and went to bed, where she lay watching the room pulse and felt she might puke. But the burpy, seafaring feeling soon morphed to one of complete paralysis. Dawn was nailed down, her mind pouring with cartoons.

Laurel stepped in to turn the light off. When she shut the door, Dawn woke with a jerk. She stared into the darkness and a swell of noises built up around her, rock music and an ambient collision of voices. She thought it was the neighbors but when she closed her eyes, she realized the noises were coming from inside her head. And she saw something: a darkened room full of people. It was a bar, she realized. Everyone was talking or dancing, a dim red light pressing down on them.

They were only vague shapes, a whole swarm of them. When Dawn focused on a single face, it moved away too quickly—ecstatically—to the beat. It was almost frightening, their thumping joy. Everyone was moving. Everyone was out of focus. Everyone but Dawn's parents. And in that moment she knew. Even before her mother spotted her father in the crowd, she knew she was watching the night of her conception.

Her mom stood at the bar, staring at her dad from across the room. She wore a strong-shouldered blazer, her short hair bleached white. When he waved, she strode over to him. His friends stepped away as she approached, almost as if they were afraid of her. Then he grinned sheepishly. He seemed to be wearing eyeliner. He handed her his beer and she took a long drink, handing it back with a carnal smile. They were so young and thin, Dawn observed.

So *attractive*. Her mom tucked a strand of her dad's hair behind his ear. She said he looked good. Then she kissed him. It was a greedy, penetrating kiss and he accepted it, clutching her jaw.

Dawn was wary of these visualizations. They felt imported, not of her design: *real*. The mouth of history was opening. *This is no dream,* she thought.

Again her mom kissed her dad and then drew her mouth away, as if to see the effect. He looked ambivalent suddenly. He rubbed his chin.

Her mom hardly blinked. She smoldered with certainty, her body tipping toward him, offering itself. It didn't seem like a trick. It seemed like love. Her mom had damp eyes and a muscular mouth. It was a beautiful combination of will and passion, Dawn thought.

Her dad said nothing but his face was a mess of feeling. His hands moved oddly over her mom's body, almost appraisingly. *God,* Dawn thought. *He has never been able to express himself.* But then she realized he was. He always had been. Even in 1986. His face said everything he couldn't.

When Watched

Theo wanted to run away. She crouched beside the cafeteria garbage can and planned her disappearance, eating a jelly sandwich and then a cookie, quickly so that no one could ask for a piece. She pictured her mother Linda sobbing onto a pillow, waiting for the phone to ring, expecting the worst. And then begging on her hands and knees for God to bring her daughter back, even though Linda had never shown any interest in God. On TV people who asked God for things were in jail or they had cancer. They seemed desperate to Theo and she took great pleasure in pitying them. Theo envisioned her classmates praying too. Even the mean ones, and in her mind they were made tender by grief. She couldn't hear their prayers but she could see them. For them praying was the act of remembering everything she had ever done in public. Theo licking a popsicle. Theo drawing a monkey on lined notebook paper. Theo in denim overalls with her arms folded, refusing to recite times tables in front of the class.

Theo felt buzzed. She sauntered past a long line of kids waiting with orange trays. Then past exhausted lunch ladies who leaned with big drippy spoons over vats of hot meat in sauce. Theo sat with a thud next to Charlie, a gentle boy with long dirty hair and a runny nose. He gulped from a small red carton of milk and then slammed it down on the beige Formica table, gasping for breath and then coughing.

"I have a boyfriend," Theo announced, chewing her index finger. She could say anything; she would be gone soon.

"I thought I was your boyfriend."

"Well you're not." She spread her hands flat on the sticky table. "He comes to my house every day," she said and Charlie leaned in, pawing his nose, entranced by her certainty. "Then we you know," she said, though Charlie didn't and neither did she. Theo understood sex as a session of spirited naked wrestling that took place when a man with wild charm talked a woman into his room. Women on TV didn't like sex. They were never ready unless they had been molested by their uncle or their brother when they were kids. And then their whole sense of readiness was thrown off kilter and they said yes to everyone. Theo couldn't wait to be not ready, to say no please no and be savagely undressed.

She sat thrilled by her fib, eyes darting around the cafeteria. Theo didn't like to talk to anyone besides Charlie but she felt free to look long and hard at anyone she pleased. Charlie stared at his food, mystified, letting mucus run into his mouth. "Do you kiss?" he asked and took a big bite of fish patty.

"Yes."

"Kissing is fostrup," Charlie whispered through his food.

"What?" Theo demanded.

"Fostruppuz."

"I can't hear you!" Theo jabbed him in the ribs and his bowed face shot up.

"Kissing is for strippers!" he blurted and then looked back down at his food. Theo considered this. She imagined a stripper kissing a fully dressed man with her tongue. The two were quiet for a while.

"My mom doesn't want you to come over anymore," Theo said.

"Why?"

"Because she really hates you a lot," she said and watched him want to cry. He breathed heavily through his open mouth, which smelled like cloudy goldfish water. His mother Sandy never closed her mouth either and Theo hated when she got close, filling the air between their faces with gross little wafts of whatever she had eaten that day. Sandy was barrel-shaped with boobs like elf shoes. She had a stripe of hard black hairs above her lips and Theo couldn't help but stare. "Why do you have a mustache?" she had blurted one night during dinner at their house, though she really wanted to say: "You have a mustache." She had been pleased with her choice of words, knowing that insults from children were always more forgivable when posed as questions. Who did Sandy think she was, with her prickly whiskers and stained sweaters, stinking up the dishes and the air and her own son? Theo felt that someone had to embarrass her. Someone had to let her know who she was.

"When you get older, you get hair in all kinds of places. Just you wait. It's perfectly normal," Sandy assured with a huge hard smile and set her fork down as if to keep from using it violently. Theo eyed the little hairs all night, as they twitched like roach legs with each bite. She pushed her spinach into careful gray islands and spoke only to the mustache when she asked Sandy to bring her home.

———

Theo sat bent over a blue egg crate full of dirty plastic toys when Linda appeared in the doorway. Her mother often stopped and stood in the doorway but rarely did she go into Theo's room. She stopped to make sure Theo wasn't dead or destroying something valuable and then left.

"What are you doing?" she asked the backside of her daughter.

Without turning, Theo pointed to a facedown rag doll.

"She had sex with her best friend's husband," Theo said, gnawing the stiff lesions around her fingernails. "Her best friend came home and they were taking a bubble bath with candles. She said I knew it you bastard and got a divorce."

"I need you to zip me." Linda walked to the front of her daughter. She knelt in a backless green dress that brought out the veins on her breasts. Theo raised the zipper to the base of her spine. Her mother was sweating; she always radiated heat before she went out at night.

"Don't trash my room while I'm gone," she said and Theo stiffened, glowing with panic. But this was the sort of fright she enjoyed. Because Linda rarely snapped and Theo wished she would more often. Her mother had a maddening way of composing herself quietly, sitting in bed touching her hair instead of slapping her daughter. Theo tried to imagine the places her mother went at night and who she showed her underwear to. Men sometimes slept at the apartment and in the morning Theo stared, amazed by how comfortable these strangers were in her house. They winked at her while gathering their belongings or sipping coffee. One man gave her a handful of coins and pocket dirt. He said she was a very serious child and could one day make a fine judge if she cared to.

Those mornings her mother was a hideous flirt, letting her robe fall from one shoulder, her whole body blushing. She would stand at the stove scrambling eggs and fondling her weird dangly earrings, sometimes glancing over one shoulder, grinning.

And Theo would eat her cereal solemnly. She hated her mother's controlled tone and hoped something would disrupt it. Maybe a forearm burn at the stove or an unrestrained fart. But nothing like this ever happened. Linda maintained her measured display of arousal. Maybe she had been molested as a child. Theo thought yes, certainly.

Linda patted her high hump of gelled hair and Theo pressed her face down onto her mother's lap. She tried to be her heaviest self, to be immovable, but Linda pulled one hand through her hair and she softened. Linda carried her to bed and sat running her fingernails up and down Theo's back. Theo hated how she could be wooed into a relaxed state so easily. She fell asleep enraged.

Theo dreamt deeply of revenge, drowning the guinea pig of a girl she particularly disliked. She considered the possibility of jail time and jerked awake.

It was dark. She was alone and instantly furious, belly down and clammy in the clothes she had put on that morning: high-waisted corduroys and a T-shirt with a winking cartoon puppy on it. The crosstown bus hissed down her block and bars of light shot across the ceiling. She wanted so badly to sneak to her mother's bed, to burrow her face in Linda's warm wall of back fat. She wanted to say that her stomach hurt, even though it didn't.

Theo tiptoed to her mother's bedroom and reached beneath the massive comforter, hoping to find a shoulder or hip or hand. She listened for her mother's whistling nose. After a few seconds she realized she was alone. Theo turned on the light. Her mouth trembled as it always did before she cried, but she decided not to since there was no one there to watch.

Theo walked to the kitchen and dumped a stack of saltines onto a plate. She swung open the refrigerator and knelt before the radiant room of batteries and yogurt, then dragged her crackers one by one across a lump of butter, dropping them in rows on the plate.

She climbed back into her mother's bed and turned on the television, leaning back, pleased to discover that *Losing Sarah* was on again. Sarah was only out of her mother's sight for an instant before she vanished forever. Though missing photos were posted door-to-door and every townsperson with a flashlight joined the search, Sarah's body was found jammed into the trunk of an abandoned car. Her body was never shown, only the scene of the crime, the aftermath. A dirty street in daylight, littered with the vestiges of her last living moments: a path of blood with smears from her struggling fingers, one scuffed Mary Jane the size of a potato chip, a fistful of blonde wisps blown up into the branches of a nearby tree.

Theo's favorite part of the film came at the end, when the kidnapper was torn from his home in handcuffs and dragged through a crowd of hysterical townspeople and news reporters. He had beady eyes and pocked cheeks, his freckled scalp protruding from a ring of frizzy red curls. Sarah's father launched his body onto the criminal, spitting and weeping onto him, yanking his carroty hair. Theo watched fixedly as he cowered on the pavement; she felt she had participated in both his capture and his crime.

Theo imagined where a kidnapper would hide in her apartment if he had the opportunity, if her mother left the door open. She pictured him, breathing quietly under the bed, ready to grab an ankle. How long had he been waiting so patiently? Hours and hours, she decided. Theo felt flattered that she had been chosen out of so many other gorgeous children. She wondered if it was her narrow, upturned nose or pleated jumper. Or maybe the fact that she was such a likable child, never throwing tantrums or wetting the bed. Her kidnapper was in love with her and Theo knew that his love was a kind of sickness, but she cherished this wild, wrongful affection, precisely because it could not be suppressed. Being kidnapped seemed like a compliment.

Theo envisioned her violent capture and eventual murder. Her teeny killed body: hard and discolored with rot, propped within a ring of candles in her kidnapper's apartment. He would be caught because he couldn't bear to throw her away. The smell would alert the neighbors.

Theo lifted whole crackers into her mouth, picturing her mother's face as a private investigator leaned in with the bad news, his beefy palm on her shoulder. He would be sure to tell Linda that Theo was too good for this world and promise to keep the monster behind bars. Perhaps he would add that it must have been difficult having such a beautiful daughter, that there must have been so many other men who wanted to kidnap her, what with that narrow nose, that white-blonde hair.

At the funeral, her mother would sit hunched over a fistful of sodden tissues, crying the way people try not to in public. Charlie would stand over Theo's powdered corpse, lowered into a glossy casket with her teeny fingers assembled carefully on her breast, two tough curls around one long white lily. Charlie would know that his ears were too big and he smelled too much like a neglected turtle to ever be kidnapped, as he stared down at the only friend he'd ever had. And Sandy would be there too, feeling ugly in her dress.

News reporters would barge through the crowd of inconsolable weepers, lifting their microphones to the mouths of her classmates, who said they really missed Theo and meant it. One student would read Theo's poems aloud, poems that consisted of long, thoughtful lists of her dislikes, complete with supplementary illustrations. The sobbing kid would stand before a blown-up picture of Theo in a frame inscribed with the words WE WILL NEVER FORGET. The crowd would sit hushed by every poem, touched, nodding in unison. In a variety of ways they said God her life had been hard. Even the reporters would cry and then take breaks to fix their makeup. That night on the news, they would announce that a new law had been passed to punish particularly choosy perverts in especially merciless ways. This law would be named after Theo.

Theo would spy on her body from heaven. And heaven was a great white sea of the similarly beautiful, the unlawfully adored, the stalked. Theo appreciated the promise of death and the dependable traditions that followed it. Everyone she had ever met would be at her funeral, leaning over her pink pleats in prayer. Not to say goodbye, but to say hello for the first time. A real hello, hello from her nose to her feet. With their eyes, they would reach into her perfect mouth, bright and quiet. They would dip into her hair and duck beneath her dress to see those purpled places, those finger-shaped bruises. They would analyze her marks to determine the size and placement of her kidnapper's hands, to see how she had been touched. People are able to look longer at a dead girl because they do not need permission, a dead girl does not look back when watched.

Theo grew tired of waiting for her kidnapper and decided to go find him instead. She brushed her cracker crumbs onto Linda's pillow and hurled the plate at the wall. She marched to her room, cramming her backpack with a blue carnival bear and a flashlight. She yanked the sheets half off her mattress and shattered her bedside Bambi lamp, swatting all the framed photos from the walls on her way to the front door.

Theo walked up to the roof. She sat on the cool tar, petting the yellow hairs on her shins and wondering when her mother would notice she was missing. And how long would she search for her? Would she find her in time? Theo peeked down at the street, biting her fingers, to see if any cop cars were parked outside. The orange-lit avenue was dotted with nuzzling pairs of heads and Theo spat at them. She lay on the tar the way someone would to get a suntan.

The weak line of light streaming from Theo's flashlight only reached so far, disappearing a few feet beyond her grasp. He could be here, she thought, tucked under a square of shadows. And if he was here, he would take her to a damp corner of land, overgrown with trees and shrubs. She closed her eyes to see him better. In the moonlight his boxy teeth beamed bright and white as hospital coats, his hairdo hung over one eye. The other eye was gigantic and blue; it knew every angle of her, towering loyally, possessed with love.

He explained that he'd been watching her for a while, even watched her sleep by climbing up the fire escape and squatting there for hours. He said she looked great sleeping and she felt her face heat up. "I don't snore or drool?" she asked.

"Never," he said, and with shy delight she looked up into his one lit-up eye. The man was dressed more to host a cocktail party than a kidnap. He wore a black bow tie. Moonlight pooled on the tops of his tuxedo shoes.

"Are you going to kill me?" she asked.

"I am going to put you in there." He pointed beyond tall weeds to a lake. Every star winked, every star had the heartbeat of a tiny baby shark. He carried her into the water like a fireman from a burning building. He was sure to tell her everything she was about to feel. Like a good doctor, he described what a lungful of lake water felt like.

Polaroids in the Snow

She is sitting in bed with a mug of red wine and a book. She is barely reading the book. Mostly she is thinking. Occasionally she drinks from the mug. She is thinking that she is a weak person. She is thinking that her main weakness is her fear of fighting with people. She cannot bear to fight, not with anyone, even people she hates. This means she will do anything to resolve a disagreement right away, even if it means admitting she is wrong when she is not wrong, or apologizing when she is not sorry.

Her ex-husband was not afraid of fighting. He even seemed to enjoy it a little. She decides that this is why he always got his way.

She pictures them in bed after an argument: her crying and him silent. Sometimes he would leave the room when he noticed that she was crying but most of the time he would remain in the room. She would heat up and stare into space and give lengthy imagined speeches. She would stay quiet and it was like being quiet while being pinched very hard. She would wait for him to speak, or to show some signs of longing for her to speak. But he showed no signs of longing and he continued not to speak.

Often, she first broke the silence with a few soft, inarticulate sounds. Then, with mounting panic, a herd of language followed like frightened animals. She would say she was sorry and his face would morph into a gentler face. She remembers her merging sense of relief and defeat. She feels embarrassed.

Outside it is snowing. She looks out her small window and is soothed by the great load of whiteness. One bundled man is walking slowly by, leaving a trail of dark gouges in the snow. It is coming down harder now than it was earlier, when she walked the dog. On the steps of her building someone had dropped a few Polaroids and she stopped to look at them. In one she identified an arm and half a smiling head but the other two Polaroids were entirely defaced, just marbled squares of brown and yellow.

She wonders now if her husband was also giving imagined speeches during the silences that followed their fights. She thinks a moment and decides not. She decides that he was as detached as he appeared to be. She thinks that she would not want his skill of leaving in the presence of someone. But an instant later she realizes that this is a total lie. Because she would certainly rather be like him than like her. She would certainly rather leave than be left.

She reads three lines in her book but doesn't hear them. She rereads them and the words seem to dissolve. She worries, as she always worries when this happens, that she will never be able to read again. That she will be spending the rest of life trapped in a chamber of her own thoughts, just a tortured head talking to itself. But she assures herself that these voices—her voices—always die down to a static hum. Probably, she thinks, her mind will be emptied by tomorrow, like a shaggy forest after a storm, cool and dripping and still. *Then,* she thinks, *I will be able to read.*

She puts the book down and finishes her wine. She lies on her side and begins to relax. She thinks she can only relax when she is exhausted. But she is glad to be exhausted. She likes to sleep. She likes when it comes down like an ax.

Like Baby

James arrived at Margo's apartment in the early evening. He had wet hair, which she took as a compliment, since it usually looked oily, falling in sections over his forehead.

"Hey," he said and walked right in, looking around freely, like a prospective buyer. He wore an olive army jacket like a shirt, buttoned low, a triangle of his pale chest exposed. Margo stood and watched as he perused the bookshelf, then picked up a framed photograph of herself and her sister as kids.

"There I am suffering." Margo smirked.

"This is you?"

"Yeah."

"You have a twin?"

"Yeah." She secretly loved the poolside shot. The two little red-haired girls were obviously identical, but she felt that her own face blazed out of the photograph, as if her child self knew something extra. "That's me," she said, pointing.

"Why did your parents buy you the same bathing suit?"

"If we got different gifts—like even if they were just *slightly* different—one always seemed better and we'd get in a fight. We were kind of like dogs that way." She paused. "It *was* weird though. Everyone stared at us. My mom loved it. She hated when we started looking different."

"What do you mean looking different?"

"Baby got her nose pierced and bleached her hair." Margo laughed. "It looked so bad. We were thirteen."

"Baby?"

"When she was eleven she started insisting we call her that. Her real name is Kate."

"Weird," he said, setting the frame back down.

"I think she saw people saying it to women on TV."

He laughed. "What's she like now?"

Margo couldn't think of much that had changed. At twenty-three, Baby was the same moody, protean creature. She hated sharing a face with Margo and often reasserted her desire to get a nose job once she had enough money. The two lived together but Margo had begged Baby to stay with their parents that night. "I'll do anything," she said and Baby groaned. But then after much coercing she packed a little bag and left.

"Now her hair is black," Margo said. "And she's really smart. Probably smarter than me. The thing is, she does *nothing*!"

"What do you mean nothing?"

"I mean she just watches TV. And makes *brilliant* passing remarks."

He smiled. "I know those types. There's no society for them."

"Yeah," Margo grinned. "Which is fine. But now she's on antidepressants." Her eyes narrowed. "And I'm so against it."

"You liked her better when she was depressed?"

"She didn't seem *clinically* depressed to me. I mean . . . for a shut-in who does nothing but watch TV, depression seems like an appropriate response. Taking pills just seems . . ." Margo broke off. "It's just something she's doing to be different from me."

"Everyone I know is on antidepressants," he said.

"Yeah and they're all on the *same* antidepressants," Margo chimed. "Like, as if our insides aren't particular."

"Right," he said, nodding.

"In fifty years we'll look back and find these drug treatments barbaric," Margo continued. "It's gonna get a lot more refined, I think."

"Well I won't ever take that shit."

"Me neither. But at a certain point we won't have a choice. Pharmaceuticals get in the water. People flush pills and pee them out. Hormones too."

"Hormones?"

"From birth control."

"Oh right." He looked down at his hands. "Shit."

"We treat water like it's endless," she said. "But there isn't much left."

They both tensed when she said this. Margo took a breath.

"Are you okay?" she asked.

"Yeah." He looked at her. "It just makes me think about the apocalypse."

"I know. A lot of things make me think about the apocalypse," she said, eyes wide. "I think all these women dying to get pregnant are insane."

"You don't want a baby?" He looked genuinely surprised.

"No."

He stared at her.

"Why let this stranger into your body, then into your home?" she said, wishing she could stop the speech building in her mouth. "It seems mentally ill. People never talk about the fact that babies are strangers. I mean, you don't know this person."

"But you love them. I mean, usually you love them right away."

"So why bring them to this awful place?"

He smiled. "I don't know. To meet them I guess."

This silenced Margo. She wondered if she appeared grim. James fixated on the owl wall clock and she strained to decipher his expression. The dark turn in conversation had snatched from the room the feeling that anything could happen. Margo wondered if she had imagined the flirtation to begin with.

"Do you mind if I smoke?" James asked, pulling a pack of Marlboro reds from his shirt pocket.

"No," she said. Margo despised smoking but she wanted him to have it—the thing he wanted.

James poked a cigarette between his lips and lit it with a match. "Do you wanna take the pictures?" he asked, shaking the match out.

"Okay. We should go to my room, then," Margo said, blazing with dread. She had forgotten all about the pictures. That was why he was there, she reminded herself.

James sat in front of her in Oceanography—a summer class and the very last one she needed to graduate college. She was in love with him so she said she was a photographer. It was the first thing that came to mind. She said she was putting a portfolio of portraits together and would he mind posing. Then he said "Sure" and she stood there, marveling at what had just occurred.

It didn't feel like a total lie because she had always wanted to be a photographer. And maybe, she thought, the lie would inspire her to take photography seriously and she would develop as an artist, blow everyone away. It would be like the time she was cast in *The Wizard of Oz* in high school and had to learn how to sing. Now she could sing.

In her room James began taking his clothes off without being asked to, the cigarette drooping from one side of his mouth, smoke obscuring his eyes. Margo turned on the ceiling fan and the whole room hummed. "Sorry," she said. "The air conditioner's broken."

James shrugged. He stood naked by the white brick wall. "Tell me what to do," he said and tapped ash into one cupped hand. It was shocking.

"Here," she said, handing him a mug. He promptly squashed the cigarette out and lit another, his dick hanging frankly. Margo blushed as she held the camera. Helplessly she glanced at herself in the mirror—that fearful, horny person.

"Mark of the devil," her grandfather had said to her once while drunk, petting her red hair.

"I'm not the devil," Margo shot back. She was six.

"You're not," the old man said. "But he designed you. *Twice*." He chuckled to himself and Margo just stood there, staring up into the red holes of his nose.

"Are you doing anything this summer?" she asked James. "I mean when class ends."

James nodded. "I'm going on a road trip with my friend Jack."

"You can drive?"

"Yeah."

"I can't," she confided. "I don't even wanna learn. I'm pretty sure I'd kill someone."

"No you wouldn't," he smiled. "Driving is great. You're forced to be the person you're not." Streams of smoke issued from his nose. "What about you—any plans?"

"I don't know," Margo said, staring through the lens. "Taking care of my sister I guess. She lives here."

He looked confused. She took a picture.

"She gets really depressed," Margo explained, lowering the camera from her eye. "Last summer it was much worse. She was talking about killing herself."

"Shit." James took a drag. "So your parents are *making* you live with her?"

"No. I like living with her. I mean, we argue but whenever she goes away I miss her. Last summer she stayed at this like, *loony* bin in New England. Only it sounded really great to me. Like summer camp or something." She looked down at the camera in her hands. "I remember going to Kmart and thinking I saw her. I said, Baby!" Margo looked up at him. "But I was seeing myself in a mirror. It was *me*."

"Whoa."

"It was eerie," she said. There was a pause. "Turn around," she said and snapped a picture of his broad back, the violet bruise hovering on his shoulder blade. "Try to stand up straight," she said softly and he did, seemingly without a care in the world. But when he faced her, Margo saw his vanity. Behind a wavering ribbon of smoke, James seemed to be watching her carefully.

Margo walked up to him and moved her hand across his chest. She couldn't believe what was happening. She couldn't believe that she wanted something and was now getting it. Of course, he wasn't the sort of person she could really *have*. He seemed to her like a wild thing and that was his beauty. *I'm an animal too,* she thought. *My animal loves his animal.*

It was minutes before sundown. The air was cooler. Electric blue light spread throughout the room and over his skin. Margo set the camera down.

"What time is it?" he asked.

"Seven."

"Crazy."

"I know," she said and crawled onto her bed, highly aroused. "Come here."

He did and her heart pounded. They lay by the window, the weakening blue light on their faces. Margo leaned forward and kissed him, pressing her hands to his chest. It was a long, plunging kiss. He held her face. Then they rolled around, feeling each other up, her dress hiked halfway up her body.

"You have like a porno look," he said.

"What?"

"No it's good. I like that your face can't hide its excitement."

She got on her back and stared up at him. What he said felt funny, like it wasn't his. She guessed someone had said this to him once. "I like that your face can't hide its excitement." She wondered who it was.

Margo lifted her butt and James pulled off her underwear. He looked at the lower half of her body for a moment, then walked across the room, where his jeans were on the floor. Margo watched as he pulled a condom from his back pocket and tore it open. He rolled it onto his hard-on, then walked back to the bed and pushed into her.

"Did you know this was gonna happen?" she asked.

"No," he said. "I didn't know."

In the morning, Margo put on the *White Album* and made coffee.

"It's weird that everyone likes the Beatles," James said, not unkindly, as he walked into the kitchen, his face marked by the folds of her sheets. He was dressed, his hair snarled on one side, flat and greasy on the other.

She smiled. He could've said anything. "It *is* weird." She handed him a mug of coffee and a carton of milk.

"No milk," he said, taking the mug. He sat at the table and lit a cigarette.

"I didn't think this was gonna happen," she said, smiling, sipping her coffee. "I thought I was freaking you out when I was talking about water and the end of the world."

"No," he said and dragged on the cigarette thoughtfully. "I mean, *you* weren't freaking me out but the end of the world does. I have dreams about it."

"I wish I could visit you in your dreams," she grinned. "Ob-La-Di, Ob-La-Da" started playing and she switched off the stereo.

"Mostly they're nightmares."

"Well I could protect you. I'm very brave in dreams."

"Really?"

She nodded. "Oh yeah. I'm a big hero."

The front door slammed and Baby walked in looking pale. She set her bag down and a white cat came running.

"Hi," James said.

"Hi," Baby said curtly, barely making eye contact. Her short black hair was combed sideward. She wore a ratty green dress and her chest was crowded with glinty charms on chains: a little jeweled guitar, a sneaker, an ax.

James squatted to pet the cat, his cigarette raised. The animal accepted his hand with a full-body lean, purring continuously.

"Has she been here the whole time?" James asked.

"It's a he," Baby said.

"That's Chowder," Margo said. "He was under the couch. He hates me."

"He's my cat," Baby clarified.

"Beautiful," James remarked, tickling under Chowder's chin.

"I know," Baby said, grinning. "I'm like his homely keeper."

They all laughed and James stood up. "I'm gonna go." He jabbed his cigarette out and smiled. Then he was gone.

Baby slunk over to the couch. She lay on her back and closed her eyes.

"You look awful," Margo said.

"I threw up this morning," Baby croaked. She put a round pillow on her stomach and laced her fingers over it. "I drank too much wine with Mom . . . wine and salad."

"Jesus, you can't just eat salad if you're gonna—"

"I *know*," Baby said, a weak rage gathering in her eyes. She moved the pillow and applied both hands directly to her abdomen. "I hate throwing up," she said. "You're surrendering utterly to your body and you don't get like, a baby or a turd. You get a puddle of food."

Margo laughed.

Chowder bounded up onto the couch as if it were a beach and Baby remained staring from the standpoint of a shovel. "My head is pounding," she said.

Margo sat on the edge of the sofa and patted her sister's foot. Chowder turned and glared at her. "God," she said. "He's such a little *meanie*."

"No he's not," Baby said. She looked at the cat. "He's melancholy. Because he's so smart." She extended one hand and the cat approached it, sniffing her fingertips. "He's trapped in a life that doesn't suit him."

Margo looked at the cat, then at Baby. "You're talking about yourself."

Baby said nothing but gave a shy look of agreement.

Margo moved an inch away, fully ignoring the demonic white shape between them. He had spread himself over Baby's midsection.

"So James is hot right?" Margo grinned.

"Not really."

"Yes he is. You wouldn't say he wasn't unless he *was*."

"Whatever." Baby moved the white mass onto the floor and rolled onto her side, clutching her gut.

"He's so hot," Margo said. "He even makes *smoking* look hot."

"He makes it look like breathing itself."

Margo smiled. "That's true."

The next day Margo arrived to class late with a goofy smile. She sat noisily behind James, slapping a marble notebook onto her desktop. Everyone stared. When they had regrouped, she raised the eraser end of her pencil and jabbed him gently on the shoulder.

James looked back with a flash of annoyance, then leaned forward in his chair.

Margo gawked at the back of his head. Slowly, she retracted her pencil, setting it down on the desk, where it rolled to the floor. Margo didn't reach down to get it. She hardly moved. A girl in a red skirt handed her the pencil and she took it mutely, still gawking at him, her eyes immense. Margo couldn't hear anything, only the sounds of her insides: her stomach, her heart, the blood around her brain.

When class ended, James stood quickly with averted eyes.

"Hey," she said loudly.

"Hi," he said and smiled. It was a sneaky, fearful smile. He walked into the hall.

Margo shoved her notebook into her bag, walking swiftly after him. "Hey!"

"*What?*"

Margo looked stricken. "Why are you being weird?"

"I'm not," he said with another unpleasant smile. "I have somewhere to be."

Margo stopped walking. She watched him reach the end of the hallway and turn the corner without looking back. Then she leaned against the wall and slid to the floor, crowds of loud people passing obliviously. It had happened so fast, his retreat. *And now everything will be slow,* Margo thought. *This feeling. It could last forever.*

She left the building and felt violent toward strolling people. Businessmen passed one by one, talking loudly into their headsets. She kept being caught off guard by an inviting face that wasn't for her. It was confusing and humiliating. *Every place is like an airport,* she thought.

Margo acquired a large bag of corn chips. When she got home the apartment was empty, save for Chowder, who sat meowing by the bathroom door. It was open a bit, white light pouring onto the floor. Margo approached the door and saw something else, the edge of a dark shape, rocking slightly. "Baby?" She gave the door a push and stood staring.

A black dress on a wire hanger hung from the shower rod, blowing subtly in the breeze of an open window.

Margo looked down at the cat and cried. They were the expressionless tears of someone who rarely wept—who hated to. She walked to the couch and threw herself down.

The window screeched open and Baby stepped inside with a towel over her shoulders. She wore a green bikini and circular black frames with cola-colored lenses. Her skin glistened with oil.

"What the shit?" Margo demanded.

"I was sunning myself," Baby said, removing her glasses.

"Since when do you *sun* yourself?" Margo said, cutting her eyes.

"Since now. What do you care?"

"I was worried!"

"Calm down. I was just on the fire escape."

"Well I didn't know that. You're always here!" Margo said, pointing to the spot she occupied. "And anyway, we *burn*."

"Not if exposure is gradual," Baby said. "I'm being very careful."

"Your shoulders look red."

"They're not."

Margo stormed off. She brought the corn chips to bed and ate them slowly, staring into space, weary with thought. She sensed in that moment that she would never be an adult, not in the manner she had envisioned for herself as a child. *This is never going to end,* she thought. *All this wanting.*

Baby came in and sat at the foot of the bed. "Are you seriously mad at me?"

"No."

"Are you hungry? Do you want some real food?" A rare sweetness had entered Baby's voice.

Margo greeted the alien tone with a weak smile. "Hunger isn't even the word," she said. "I'm just really interested in food." Then her face morphed back into a mask of pain and she punched the bed, startling her sister.

"What happened?"

"It doesn't matter." Margo lay on her side. "I don't know what happened. We had such a good time. I mean, I *know* he had a good time."

"Maybe he met someone else."

"In a day?"

"Guys are always weird after."

"But we were just getting started."

"Guys don't wanna get started. They want to end it and move on to someone else."

"Stop telling me what guys are like. I know what they're like." Margo sat up. "You have a sunburn."

"I know."

Margo wished in that moment that she were more like Baby, who'd never had much of an appetite for boys. Her sister just wanted a quiet room to watch television in. That or she wanted to die. Margo was never sure which it was.

"Why don't you ever go on dates?" Margo asked.

"Because I need space."

"For the rest of your life?"

"Fuck you."

"What if you're gay?"

"I am *not* gay." Baby gaped in outrage. "If I was gay, wouldn't you be too?"

"Not necessarily." Margo stared into space. "What about that guy Aaron who lives downstairs? Would you date him? He's like, *obsessed* with you."

"I'm so much smarter than him," Baby said. "And he doesn't even know it. That's part of his stupidity."

Margo repositioned her pillow and noticed it was covered in cat hair. "What the shit?" She began picking little white hairs off the faded blue fabric, one by one. "Chowder is *not* allowed in here!"

"You have to close your door," Baby said, the familiar shade of scorn resurfacing in her voice.

Margo stopped grooming the pillow, the beginnings of a

sob dimpling her chin. "Do you think anyone will ever love me?" she asked.

"Yeah. But you'll probably be too busy doing something stupid to notice."

"Be nice to me!" Margo said, her eyes welling with tears.

"Okay." Baby patted her shoulder. "I'm sorry."

Margo seized the pillow and threw it onto the floor. "I don't see how I can go back to class," she said. "I might strangle him. There's *no* kind of violence that doesn't seem appropriate."

Baby laughed. "Men are just shifty," she said uselessly. "I mean, their desires are."

Margo had entered a grim trance. "Desire is too grand a word for what men experience."

"What did he say exactly?"

"I said hey and he said *what?*" Margo said with mock disgust, her face reanimating. "Like I had appeared on his doorstep with like, his *name* carved into my neck." Margo sighed. She lay back down. "God. Why do we have consciousness?" she said.

"It was probably just a mutation that kept evolving." Baby moved the bag of chips onto the floor and lay next to her sister. "I don't know." She pulled the sheet up over them.

"I thought you were dead," Margo said.

Baby stiffened. A small silence followed. "I'm not gonna do that," she said finally, in her chilly way.

Margo looked sideward at her sister. "It would be a mistake," she said carefully.

"I know."

"I mean a corpse can't see itself lying there. It's a show for everyone but you."

"Please shut up," Baby said evenly. "I was never showing off. It wasn't like that."

"What was it like?"

Baby softened. "It was like . . . I just couldn't stop thinking about it. *How* I would do it. *When* I would do it. I feel like if I ever *did* do it, it would be to stop thinking about doing it."

"So why didn't you?"

"I don't know. I couldn't deal with someone finding me. I kept wishing there was some way to off myself and then dispose of the body."

"Well I certainly wouldn't want to find you."

"Well I wouldn't want you to look through my room and sell my stuff," Baby snapped. "There's actually a lot of preparation that goes into suicide if you care—and I *do* care. But I'm lazy so I kept putting it off."

"Maybe because you wanted to live."

"No. It was the laziness. Also the cat."

They both looked at Chowder, who sat at the foot of the bed, purring ominously. "He loves you," Margo said.

"Please. Cats don't *love* anyone. He hates me the least."

"So how would you do it?"

"I'm not discussing this with you."

"With a gun?"

"No. People fuck that up all the time. Then you wind up with like, half a face." Baby looked thoroughly at the ceiling. "I would jump off a building," she said finally, almost serenely.

"*Why?*" Margo said. She looked slapped.

"Because it's fast. You can't change your mind."

"I would *want* to be able to change my mind."

"Because you don't want to die."

"Yeah, I don't. And I don't think it's *cool* to want to die. I don't think you're *cool*."

"I don't either."

"Well good."

They were quiet then, blinking at the ceiling with their same eyes.

"I was reading that the Aztecs took your heart out when you died and weighed it," Baby said, finally. "To determine where you were going in the afterlife."

Margo made a face. "I wouldn't want anyone to do that to me."

"I think it's a little bit beautiful," Baby said, touching the crowd of charms on her chest. "I wonder what it's like to be gone."

"Probably not much of an experience."

"Yeah. It's like the *opposite* of an experience." Baby rubbed the little jeweled guitar, then the ax.

"Do you think there's enough time left on earth?" Margo asked. "I mean to have a whole life?"

They made sideward eye contact.

"I think so," Baby said. "Maybe *just* enough."

"I want to be an artist."

"So be one."

"But I feel so behind," Margo said, a tear rolling down her cheek. "I wish time would slow down."

"Well it won't."

"I don't know . . . time can be slow."

"Like when?"

"When you're in pain," Margo said quickly. Her eyes narrowed adamantly. "Or when you're seeing something for the first time."

"Right." Baby nodded. "When you feel like a *kid*."

Margo looked at Baby and saw her at every age—every era of their face. A great wave of fondness swelled between them. It was positively ancient, their love, and a little excruciating.

Sunlight quivered on the bed. They went on blinking at each other and the passing minutes seemed to fatten. "Stay like that," Margo said and reached for her camera.

"You should *ask*," Baby said. "And the answer is no." But then she looked up—right into the camera.

A Career

As a child he loved to sing. He was always singing and even writing down some of his songs. In college, he liked to draw and did so when he should have been sleeping. It was the only time left in the day for him. He worked two jobs in addition to his classes. He majored in art but somehow this seems irrelevant because it didn't make a difference. There was so little time and he was always so tired. But for years he drew anyway because it gave him pleasure. He drew the things in his room and the people he had crushes on. And whenever he met someone, he explained that he was an artist. He pulled out his sketchbook and watched the person flip through it. He watched their eyes. No one ever looked impressed, though a girl once said, "Wow." But he sensed she was lying.

After college he had many jobs. He worked in an office and he worked at a restaurant. He also did some babysitting. But he did not draw and he did not sing. He had trouble sleeping but no longer filled the time creatively. He just blinked in the dark. For years and years, he was blinking.

Now he is a writer and he is writing. Right now he is writing this story. His husband is cooking dinner. He can smell the meat cooking and he can feel his husband's anger to be cooking dinner alone. But his husband is the better cook. They have both acknowledged this fact. They have even laughed about it. Still his husband is resentful. He thinks his husband will always be resentful because his husband is better at so many things. This is why their relationship is withering.

Some people can fully engage in unhappy careers, he thinks. *For years they can do this, their whole lives*. His husband is this way, an unhappy lawyer, though a *good* lawyer. He thinks that he could never be like his husband, good at something he hated. He thinks that he is not even very good at the things he loves. But this is a little bit of a lie because he holds a certain pride. He loves the songs he sang as a boy and all the drawings. He has been so many people. *And all in the service of becoming me*, he thinks proudly. He loves his writing. He loves writing this now. Always he is waiting to be alone to write. *So I must like writing more than people*, he thinks. *More than my husband*.

His husband wishes he made more money and his family feels the same. They think he is delusional, calling himself a writer. It feels a lot like hate, the things they say. *They don't understand*, he thinks. *They can't imagine doing the same thing every day for hours simply because you're compelled, though you're not getting paid*.

"That is not a career," his mother has said.

"Think of religion," he said in response. "It's like that. I have *visions*." But this only enraged his mother.

He thinks that if only he could write all day alone, if only he were not always drenched in the anger of his mother and his husband, then he could arrange some semblance of a writing career. *I need some fame,* he thinks. And he writes these words very slowly. Then he hears his name. He sets down his pen. "Coming!" he says and walks through the door.

Pleasure Kid

"You're like a radiant corpse," she said to the man in her bed. She had wanted to say it for days.

"I know," he said brightly, looking up from his book. He was older than she was. "I get exhausted," he explained. "I really do. But then I get excited."

"Then you forget your body," she added.

"I really do," he smiled.

"You'll be on your deathbed," she said. "And then you'll get excited."

"And then I'll live for ten more years," he said, returning to his book.

She chucked her head back with a laugh. "You'll be like, I forgot to die."

He laughed too. He liked her cavalier attitude toward death— his death. Perversely it relaxed him.

She moved the sheet off her naked chest and wanted to kiss him but instead stared, which felt tantric—a slow burn.

He didn't mind being stared at. He felt the measured heat of her gaze and soaked it up like sunshine. Being loved—it was exactly like being at the beach. She was the sun and the ocean and the hot sand too, enclosing him in airy pressure.

She went on staring with her head on its side. She could tell he hadn't been handsome as a younger guy. But age had pushed his face into another dimension. He was handsome now. It was so often like this for funny-looking young men, she thought. Funny looked better later—rotting.

And it was just the opposite for baby-faced heartbreakers. They aged into ugly guys, she thought. All of them did. Because their perfect soft beauty wore down and all you could see was that it was gone. *They age like women . . . old peaches,* she thought, smiling wide.

He wasn't looking at her but he could hear the wet sound of her teeth being revealed. It was like a wolf breaking out of a child's face.

"Tell me about acid," she said because she'd never done it. She really wanted to but feared the things she'd do, slice her arm open or just stare into the mirror and into herself, going permanently insane.

"I already did."

"Tell me again. Tell me about looking at money."

"Well I remember looking at a dollar—the pyramid. It seemed like a religion." He set his book down. "This one guy who wasn't tripping—he was leading us—he decided we should eat pizza. And it was the kind of pizza with bubbles—you know, like airholes. So it looked like it was happening in front of us."

"Happening in front of you?"

"When you're tripping nothing is still so it wasn't just a pizza that had a few bubbles—it was like it was bubbling right there. Like it was the surface of Mars blowing up. And you would no more think about eating this thing than you would think about throwing your face down on lava and licking. It was the craziest thought in the world. So we were like scared children and of course this guy was laughing."

She smiled giddily, loving the story and his face as he told it. And she knew it was a kind of sickness, how she fell so hard and wore her weird heart on her sleeve like a little hungry roach. "I love that you did so many drugs," she said and felt like a moron. What she meant was "I love you."

"I never wanted to be anything," he said. "I just wanted to feel good."

She nodded and thought to herself that he was still living that life.

"I was a pleasure kid," he said.

She smiled. "I don't know if I am."

"I think you are."

"I might be a masochist."

"No." He shook his head as if to say that he had fucked many young masochists and was therefore an expert. "You like to feel good," he commented.

She lay there and considered her own existence, coating and enslaving her. Did she like to feel good? Sure. Good and then blank. She loved this man and would soon feel nothing for him. Even in the heat of her love she could feel the devil peering, waiting to enter her. *The devil is blankness,* she thought, hating what she contained. It was why she didn't want to do acid. Evil was too close. It lived in her cells and yearned to sing.

He was getting tired. He set his book down and looked into her blinking eyes. Then at once she asked: "Do you love me?"

"Yes."

"Really and truly?"

"Deeply and terribly."

She smiled like a fiend and he joined her there. Then, "Look at your hair," he said, giving it a stroke. "It's so *brown*."

Her smile fell. "What does that mean?"

"It's unaltered by time," he clarified. "A tree full of leaves!"

"Oh." She grinned then, happy to be a tree and a full one. Though it was certainly strange to be stroked for having lived less. And stranger to love him for having lived more.

Her gaze seesawed around the room and landed on a *Ghostbusters* DVD. It lived with the books on a nearby shelf, like it was hiding.

"You like Bill Murray?" she asked.

"What?"

She pointed to the DVD.

"Oh. Someone left that here."

"I would watch it. I like Bill Murray," she said, cocking her head at the bookshelf as if it were Bill himself. "He's looked the same for twenty years. I mean old but never *older*."

"I know," the man grinned. "He's like my apartment."

That made her laugh. Then she settled her face into the crook of his neck and felt how awake she was.

He switched off the light.

"Do you still love me?" she said.

"Since a moment ago?"

"Do you?"

"Yes."

"How can you be sure?"

"It's the last thing I think about before I go to sleep," he said. And then he did.

She exhaled. It was such a good answer. Her heart thumped against his dreaming body and she wanted desperately to join

him there. She had read that people sleeping in the same bed—
people in love—could quite literally inhabit the same dream.

But she wanted a cigarette badly. The door called to her. And
soon, without even really deciding to, she was walking toward it.

Outside the air was soft on her legs as she walked, lit cigarette in hand. It was the way she wished she felt in the morning
but only felt at night, full of intelligence and curiosity. Not
optimistic—not at all—just focused and hungry and on a path.

She stopped outside a bar and lingered in the red light,
flicking her cigarette into a dark puddle and lighting another. It
was then that she noticed someone—a small person—walking
toward her. It was a child, a little boy, getting nearer and nearer.
Soon he stood very close and said, "Hi."

She took a step back, then smiled with fear and wonder.
"Are you alright?" she asked.

The boy said "Yes" with a kind of adult conviction. It made
her stare.

"Where's your mom?"

"She's at home."

Her gaze lingered. He looked so relaxed.

"She's always home," he continued. "I was born in the
bathtub."

"Oh I've heard of that."

"When I was out of her my mom said what is it? And my
dad said a baby." The boy laughed and laughed at himself. When
she joined in, his laugh got even more hysterical.

They caught their breath and were quiet a moment. "How
old are you?" She squinted.

"Nine," he said flatly, as if feeling no connection to the
number.

"I remember nine," she grinned. "It was a good year."

He looked into her eyes very deeply and she shifted in her daisy dress and tennis shoes. Then suddenly, as if he'd heard a bell, the boy backed away, said "Bye," and walked into the bar.

She stood there a second dumbfounded, then walked toward one of the grimy windows. Inside she saw the boy standing next to a stool with a man on it. She felt certain it was his father. It had to be.

Jabbing her cigarette out on the brick wall, she had a vision of the boy as a grown man, kind of fucked up from spending night after night with his dad at a bar. She figured he would live in bars though he hated them, the dark crib of his life. *You never stop being nine,* she thought and felt like a genius. It was thrilling when she had an idea and it felt true. Some back door in her heart flew open and she had the sensation of leaving the ground, for a second anyway.

But no, not everyone was permanently nine, she decided. Some people were four. Others fifteen. *And all of us walking around with our older faces, relating as adults but feeling like children,* she thought. It was why actual children looked like celebrities— spiritual celebrities. They were so full of truth, she thought, and not just their own. It was the great secret of humanity and it whirled in their eyes.

She had a bunch more cigarettes as she walked on. She felt the air kissing her ears and neck and thanked God for it. She could only thank God for a few things, the things that were always good to her. Because otherwise God seemed to be jerking off on a hill somewhere with gleaming eyes, watching her fuck up. But the *air* was good, it always was. And the moon was good. So good. Even the rats were good the way they waddled with such speed—such *desire*. "I love you," she whispered. To all rats.

She went back to the man's apartment with a racing heart

and took all her clothes off, then crawled into bed. She had used his key so as not to wake him but he did stir when she started climbing over him, kissing up the front of his T-shirt.

He laughed in a groggy way and stuck one hand in the mess of her hair.

"I want you so bad," she muttered into his shirt.

"But you have me," he said, sitting up.

The light stayed off but moonlight from the window showed her what his face was doing. He was looking at her like she was a puppy who had eaten all his shoes. And she felt like one.

She sat up and he held her face in his hands. She was so beautiful, he thought. But beautiful like a junkie, all wild and skinny and freaked out. "What's going on?" he asked.

"I don't know. I feel funny. I don't want to lose you."

"Why would you lose me?"

"Because we're fucking."

"So?"

"Everyone who fucks someone stops fucking them at some point. And then they start fucking someone else."

"Do you want to fuck someone else?"

"No! But it's inevitable, right? One day one of us'll wake up an—"

"Don't do this."

"Okay." She took a breath. "Wait. Don't do what?"

"Tamper with perfection."

She stared a second, then nodded. "Okay."

He rubbed his eyelids and sighed. "Like every time I've become obsessed with the I Ching it becomes sort of *loathsome*."

"That's such a weird thing to say. I don't even know what you mean."

"I just mean you shouldn't think so much . . . about chance."

"Tell me about acid."

"No."

"Please."

"God." He shook his head. *"Why?"*

"I don't know. Just tell me."

"Well . . . it's like living in a poem," he said, relaxing into his pleasure. "It's cartoon and allegory . . . and the allegory goes as deep as you do."

"That's beautiful."

"It really is. You should do it already."

"No. I think I just like hearing about it."

He squinted at her. "You're a strange creature," he said, grasping her naked arm and giving it a squeeze.

"You think we'll love each other for a while?" she asked.

"Yes," he grinned. "Absolutely."

"You could die while fucking me. I mean doesn't that happen?"

"What?"

"When you do Viagra."

"I don't do it that much." He started stroking her arm. "I think you're gonna have me for longer than you expect. I'm gonna be like a telephone hanging around . . . there'll be nothing left, just this voice that's me that won't go away," he said.

It made her laugh. Then a long pause. Then she said, "Why do you like me? I'm such a grump."

"That's what I'm into."

"And I'm stupid."

"You are not."

"I can't remember the things I'm supposed to and you *know* it. My mind gets crowded with other things . . ."

"I love your mind. It's not some dumb grove where all the trees look the same."

She looked at him then and thought that he could've been anything he wanted. A poet, maybe, or a filmmaker or a novelist. But she was glad he wasn't any of those things. She was glad he was lying there in the moonlight, a big sexy nobody who could've been somebody. There was something so rich about it.

"Just enjoy this," he said.

"Because it's gonna end?"

"No. Because it's *good*." He shook his head with a little smile. "You're so morbid."

"I thought everyone was."

"Not like this." He put his hand over her heart and felt its mad flutter. "Breathe."

It turned her on, him telling her to breathe.

He said it again. *"Breathe."*

Paradise

Hank was on the sofa when his wife called. He hadn't moved much in an hour.

"My flight was delayed," Lenora said.

"Shit."

"Now I'm eating this really pathetic sandwich," she said and paused—maybe glaring at it. "It's weird not eating red meat. I'm now one of those people who asks if the chili has meat in it. And of course it *did*. So I was condemned to the broccoli and cheese soup. Then I got really wild and bought the Tuscan turkey sub—which is all language. It's really just the worst kind of turkey."

"The turkey that's really bologna."

"Exactly."

They were quiet a second, a low snarl of static between them.

"A lot of other people are on their phones," Lenora said. "It's how we wait. We *evacuate*." She paused quite vividly this time. Hank saw her cool blue eyes darting around the fluorescent hall of space.

"Anyone who isn't on their phone is *eating*," she said

disgustedly. "Couples mostly, but none of them are looking at each other. Eating has become this . . . grim religious practice."

Hank laughed. "I love you."

"There's a big neon sign that says toasty—bread that's going bad that's been toasted."

"I wish I was there with you."

"No you don't." Lenora took a breath as if she were about to say more but didn't. She was prone to exactly this sort of pause in a conversation as she was often distracted.

"Did you hear from Tom?" Hank asked. Tom was Lenora's agent. She had sent him the first half of her new manuscript, a novel about a female drug mule called *The Donkey Show*.

Lenora had spent the past year meeting with an actual drug mule—Angie—for research. She had read an article about the drug bust online and grew very curious about the sort of woman who boards an afternoon plane with giant packets of heroin stuffed up into the chamber of her vagina. Lenora became obsessed with Angie and soon began visiting her in jail with a tape recorder.

Secretly it made Hank a little sick.

"He loved it," she said.

"What? Why didn't you tell me?"

"I just did."

"But I had to ask."

"He said it was satisfying." She let out a huff.

"Oh come on. Who cares what he *said*?"

"It was sleazy," she said and resumed her distracted silence, which seemed now to contain annoyance.

"What are you thinking?" he asked.

She paused a second more. "That I should try to do some work while I'm stuck here. I have that contest I'm judging."

"The stories?"

"Yeah."

He scratched some dried food off the thigh of his jeans, flicked it into the air. "I love you," he said. "I'm sorry you're stuck there."

"It's actually kind of nice. I like that nobody knows who I am—I *like* being nobody." She went quiet again. "I'll call you later."

"Okay. Tell your mom uh—tell her hello."

"Hello?"

"Well. Give her my love."

"She might not remember you."

He blinked into space.

"Hank, she hardly recognizes *me*."

"Tell her anyway," he said, weirdly hurt.

"I will."

Hank hung up and sank back into the sofa, looking around. Before him hung an oil painting of three milk cartons filled with yellow and orange roses. It didn't give him any sort of feeling—never had.

Everything they owned came from an antique store, which seemed eerie to him, like they had no history. He felt like a visitor in the home of another man—a very important man who wrote book after book and fucked Lenora constantly.

Dazedly he pictured her naked chest, soft with a pale explosion of freckles and one red birthmark that she loathed. It lived under one of her breasts and resembled a little spoon. "I love it," he would say to her in bed, putting his face near the spoon. Then she'd roll her whole naked self away, pull the sheet up, and groan.

Hank sat there picturing it—the spoon. The moment of seeing it before she turned. He wondered what Lenora was thinking about at that moment. *Her mother? Another man? Existence?*

The love always came this way—like a mallet. And then he saw stars. It didn't feel good—the pictures that hovered at the front of his skull: Lenora kissing up the zipper of his jeans, then peeking up to say what she said once, four years ago: "I can't believe I can have this."

"What?"

"*You.*"

Hank woke up an hour later. He ran his tongue over the lemony fur on his teeth and swallowed—revolted, then shut his eyes again and lay there, tipping in and out of consciousness.

In a fog he observed whole hours fleeing his life forever. He kept picturing what he would do if he could move. Make a roast beef sandwich with mustard. Masturbate. Write seventy pages without stopping. Or pee—suddenly he really had to. He ignored the urge but it waged on and on and soon he had a vision of himself soaking the sofa.

I'm a neglected dog, he thought and then realized that in this scenario he was also the abusive owner.

Lenora had a theory about dog training that he never forgot. "You give them a treat when they're good," she said. "But only *sometimes*. No dog should be rewarded every time."

Hank considered the chronic hope of a dog trained this way, a dog made to wonder: *Will she give it to me now? How bout now?* It seemed cruel to melt a being down like that—to nothing but desire.

Outside a bottle shattered and he was grateful for it. They lived on Riverside Drive and generally there was no one in sight, just joggers—haggard, anorexic ones. Maybe there were some kids out there, he thought, a smile on his lips. *Getting tanked.*

Hank glared down at his body, then ordered himself to stand. He felt tired, flabby and separate from the universe. Like an athlete without a team. Or a sport.

The apartment was dark and manicured, a long hall with the occasional foreign object on a shelf: an eel trap, a ceremonial African hat, a yellow-eyed devil in a shadow box. It seemed so many steps to the bathroom.

Hank had read that most depressed people didn't know they were depressed, which fascinated him—being that he was so acutely aware of his own depression. *This should feel good,* he thought when the arc of urine crashed into the toilet. *It doesn't.*

He didn't wash his hands. He ran a green comb through his hair and turned before the mirror, examining his stomach in profile—the low mound. Then he gazed at his mouth, which had a slight duck quality. *Quack,* he thought, shutting his lips. *Quack, quack.*

It was a face that had been called strange as many times as it had been called—not *handsome,* not that word—but as many times as it had been kissed.

Hank returned to the sofa and crawled onto it. Loneliness stabbed him all over. *But what is it called when your loneliness is worse around other people?* He shut his eyes. *Surely there's some long German word for that.*

Hank wished he were writing. He had written one good book but the world didn't think so. Then he wrote another book but he didn't love it and neither did the world. Now he was thirty-nine. He thought about his age every day. He also thought he would never write again.

He wondered how many other people were lying miserably on sofas in Manhattan. *A fucking lot,* he thought. Night had come down through the windows and across the room in long furry slabs. It made him understand suicide—the darkness did. A desire to take the night and put it inside oneself—that made complete sense.

Hank sat up and imagined himself dead on the blonde wood floor. He let out a big laugh. *Death is just that,* he thought. *A punch line.*

What's the joke? he imagined someone might ask.

Your life is the joke.

Then he remembered something—a poem. He thought of the poem a lot—more than he thought of the woman who had written it, a woman he had dated in his twenties. The poem was called "Beautiful Things the Poor Can Have" and at first it made him squirm when she read it from her notebook. But by the end of it he had restrained a sob.

The poem was very literal minded—much like the poet herself. It contained a sort of grocery list of things the poor could have—beautiful things. He still remembered parts of it.

> *The poor can put their shoes on.*
> *The poor can go for a walk.*
> *The poor can say look at the moon it looks like my*
> *mother. Everyone will laugh.*
> *The poor can smoke a cigarette.*
> *The poor can have a good idea that grows in the dark.*
> *The poor can tell a lie and say sorry, that was a lie.*
> *The poor can get in bed and have a dream.*
> *The poor can wake up with a headache.*
> *The poor can shuffle to the kitchen for water and see*
> *their dog and feel okay.*

The poor can sit in a chair—their favorite chair.
The poor can look at their own hand and feel
beautiful.
The poor can have a baby and often they do.
The poor can say look at my baby. Isn't my baby
beautiful?
They can hold their baby high
show all their teeth
and know God.

Hank remembered the soft look of pride on the poet's face when she stopped reading.

"Do you like it?" she asked.

"Very much," he said.

"But do you *get* it?" she asked.

"I think so," he said and smiled. "Tell me anyway. Tell me what it means."

"It means the poor can have it all," she said. "And *do*." Then she kissed him.

The poet had been very poor and at that time he had been poor too. They had been poor together in a tiny apartment in Chinatown and the sex was spectacular.

Now that he was married to a wealthy woman, he wondered what that made him. Not rich exactly—but certainly not poor either. It was a little like being nobody, he thought. *Like a little vase all naked on a shelf.*

Mentally he began a list of all the things the rich could have.

Really nice doorknobs.

Rooms they don't even use.

Big closets with wooden hangers.

Duvets with duvet covers.

Weird lighting fixtures—modern sorts of chandeliers.

Fresh flowers.

Copper cooking pots.

Business associates.

Health care.

Rules about how to behave.

Privacy.

Things that are white but not dirty.

Hank thought of reaching for a pen but instead grabbed his phone and called Lenora.

"Hey," she said after the third ring, her voice a tad something.

He hesitated. "Are you smoking?"

"That's the least of my problems right now, believe me."

He went mute. She had taken such pains to quit.

"I can't explain it," she said quickly. "I bought a pack when I got off the plane. It just seemed right." She exhaled. "The blankets are so bad here. I keep adding another one. They're not that thin but seem to be made of air."

"I can't believe you're smoking."

"I don't want to be lectured," she said evenly.

"Fine." He took a gruff pause. "How's your mother?"

"You know, the same. Sweet and demonic. Like Satan pretending to be a baby."

Hank laughed. "I love you, you know that."

"I do."

"I know I've been saying that a lot. I hope you know I mean something a little different each time."

"I know."

Hank paused. "I don't want it to become meaningless."

"It won't." Lenora exhaled. "Mom gave me a picture," she said, "of me as a baby. She wants me to give it to you."

"That's sweet."

"I don't think so," Lenora sniffed. "She kept saying how much she loved it when I was a baby and suddenly I realized why. I thought oh, you didn't want to *meet* me."

"Can she hear you right now?"

"I don't care. She's hardly spoken to me. I went out for hours, she didn't even notice."

"Where did you go?"

"Walmart. I just walked around so long that I started thinking what a great deal."

"Jesus."

"I know. Arlington's a toilet. Always has been."

"Honey, I'm sorry."

"It's okay. I'm not depressed. I'm actually kind of inspired. It's not that I want to be a better person." She paused. "I just don't want to be like my mother."

He laughed.

"I know she's losing her shit—I mean I get that. But she was always a jerk so there's nothing really to *grieve*."

"What time are you bringing her to the place tomorrow?"

"It's called Fern Valley."

"Sounds like a cemetery."

"*Well*," she said smokily, a smile in her voice.

He pictured her staring out a window, which was exactly what she was doing.

"And now all this stuff I wasn't allowed to *touch* as a kid is being thrown out," she said. "It's all over the lawn. People have been taking things."

"Don't you want any of that stuff?"

"No."

"I miss you," he said, then regretted it.

"I'll be back tomorrow."

"Do you miss me?"

"I've been gone for less than a day. So no."

He was quiet a second. "Sometimes I hate your honesty."

"I thought you missed me."

"I *do*."

"Well." She took a long drag. "This is me."

The next day Lenora arrived at their door with a bruisey look of exhaustion around her eyes, brown hair tucked back at the ears. She wore a long sand-colored coat and knee-high leather boots. Hank kissed her on the mouth, tasted mint and a cigarette. He looked into her tired eyes.

"Will you help me with this?" she asked.

Hank wheeled her suitcase in. He was always surprised by how sexy his wife was, long-limbed with a soft galaxy of freckles over her cheeks and nose. It was a little like seeing another woman every time she appeared—like she was continually being replaced by one of her more beautiful sisters.

He watched as she clacked to the hall mirror and shot it a quick glance, then went straight to her office.

Numbly he floated to the kitchen for more coffee and within minutes, she was shouting.

"What?" he yelled.

"Nothing," she said when he appeared in the doorway. She had stripped down to a sleeveless gray dress and stared fixedly at her laptop, an unlit cigarette waiting between her fingers. The room was dark, save for a standing iron lamp with a slim green shade.

"*What?*"

"This little baby novelist got a huge review in the *Times*."

Hank walked over to the laptop. "Oh him."

"He's a crashing bore, this guy. I met him once . . . years ago."

"You have such a teeming, growing shit list."

"That's what a career is." She scrolled down to the bottom of the screen. "I'm sure he *adores* my work."

"Who cares." Hank backed away from the computer. "You'll get one. You always do."

"But it won't be like this. It'll be smaller." Lenora pulled a book of matches from her purse and lit the cigarette, savagely pulling smoke into her lungs. "The best thing I could do for my career at this point is hang myself."

"That's not funny."

"It wasn't meant to be." She tugged one boot off and dropped it to the floor. "It's a *fact*. I won't be famous till I'm dead."

"But you are famous. You're famous now."

"Not like I will be." Lenora had entered an unblinking trance. "All the biographers will fight over me."

"Come on."

"That's how it works. They eat corpses—all of them do."

He stared at her. "That's a disgusting way of putting it."

"It's true though."

Hank backed out of the room, watching her as he went. Lenora was leaning forward in her cracked leather chair, shoulders gleaming in the lamplight. She stared straight ahead with a violent look of contemplation, cars going off cliffs in her eyes.

He brought his laptop to bed and Googled the poet he had dated in his twenties, Grace Lampert. In an instant he identified her on Facebook, looking rather unhealthy next to a man, presumably her husband, who also looked unwell. The image disturbed him. He clicked it shut.

Hank heard the front door slam and knew where Lenora had gone. To see the drug mule.

She returned at dusk. She walked to the bed and stared down at Hank, who lay in the same spot with his laptop balanced on his stomach, its cool blaze cast over him.

"Did you get some writing done?" she asked.

"No," he frowned. He had done nothing but masturbate. "I drank too much coffee," he said. That was true too. "Wound up paralyzed . . . grinding my teeth."

She laughed.

"How's Angie?" he asked.

"You know. Fine. Terrible."

"What do you mean?"

"I think that's what prison is like. You're fine and then you're terrible."

"Right."

"She told me a lot more about her childhood." Lenora shook her head. "It all made so much sense."

"What did?"

"The abuse."

"She was abused?"

"By her father. He beat her with a belt. She said it had a scene of the desert on it."

"Are you putting that in the book?"

"I'm not sure yet."

He stared at her. "Do you think she likes you?"

"She doesn't get a lot of visitors, Hank."

"That's not what I asked." He tried to dock her gaze with his own but it rushed away. "Does she *like* you?" he said and realized his question was really: *Does she hate you?* Because in that moment he did.

"Why would she agree to see me if she didn't like me?"

"I don't know." He threw his hands up. "Boredom? Loneliness? *Desperation?*"

Lenora cut her eyes. "What are you getting at?"

"I just wonder how she feels about her life going into a book—*your* book. Of fiction. I mean, at least if it was nonfiction—"

"I think she likes that I'm so interested," Lenora said. "Her whole life people have rejected her." She climbed into bed and pushed the laptop off his stomach, then ran one manicured finger down his chest and over his navel, pausing at the waistband.

Hank's head drained of all thought. He waited for her finger to move farther down but a second later it was gone.

She'd gotten up and opened the closet door. "John and Susan are having a party." Lenora surveyed her clothes, then withdrew a gray dress. It was almost identical to the one she was wearing.

Hank felt his excitement sputter and die—shrink down to a pit of rage. "I hate those two."

"There'll be food."

"What kind?"

"I don't know. Cheese and crackers?"

"There aren't enough cheese and crackers in the world."

She shrugged. "You don't have to go."

So of course he went.

They were both pretty drunk when they left the party. In the cab they stared out opposing windows, flat blobs of colored light flying over their faces.

"I didn't know it was Susan's birthday," Hank said. "We were the only ones without a gift."

"They live in Brooklyn. The gift is that we *came*."

He laughed.

"It was weird seeing all those guys I went to college with," Lenora said. "They all looked so different."

"You mean bad. They looked bad."

"Sort of." She patted a yawn. "They're just older—they aren't cute. Like, the *exact* thing I identified as cuteness is now gone."

"We're older too."

"I know that."

"It's so awful."

"What's so awful?"

"That we feel uglier because we *are* uglier."

"We're not ugly," Lenora said, a wound in her voice. "And maybe those guys aren't either. It was just a *shock*. Their faces looked so different without the same fat there. Or with—you know—*sudden* fat."

Hank laughed. "It didn't just appear there."

"Well that's how it looks if you haven't seen someone in a while. Like they just got hit with fat."

They both laughed, then went quiet.

Hank looked up at the moon. He said, "What were you talking to John about?"

Lenora froze in profile. "Why?"

"Because you were talking to him all night."

"So."

"You know I hate that guy."

"I still don't understand why."

"He's a creep. And he's a terrible writer."

"I didn't think his book was bad. It could be vastly *corny* at times but I thought the ending was very moving."

"I didn't get that far—I just didn't *believe* it. He's like Kevin Spacey doing Bobby Darin," Hank huffed. "Some cheap commercial rendition of hipness."

Lenora groaned.

"It's okay for me to hate this person. You hate everyone."

"No I don't."

"Yes you do. You only like him because I hate him. It's a turn-on for both of you."

"You're really starting to sound crazy."

"Right—because you're such a cheerleader for sanity."

"Why would I hit on someone in *front* of you?"

"I don't know. There's obviously something wrong with you." Hank faced the window once more, the harsh red light of surrounding cars cast over him.

"Well you were glued to what's-her-face all night. The one with the tits," Lenora hissed.

"You know her name." He turned to see her expression but she was facing the window, arms crossed. "I like her," he said. "She's nice."

"That's her thing. I'm nice! But really she's just boring."

Hank laughed in spite of himself.

"And she looks like a fetus," Lenora said. "I mean pretty but . . ."

"Unformed?" he offered.

"*Yes*. Not fully formed."

"That's the thing about fetuses."

Once home they stripped down to their underwear and climbed into bed. Hank stared sideward at the freckled contours of her body, the red spoon glowing somewhere under her lacy black bra.

She lay there like paradise itself, he thought. *An island all her own.* He rolled on his side and thought maybe the trouble with paradise was tasting it. Maybe he could only touch the door—crouch before it and wait. Maybe it was *waiting* that he loved—not Lenora.

The thought took shape and died in a matter of seconds. *I don't like waiting,* he decided. *I don't like staring this way—like a man in a museum.*

The woman he loved was the one who loved him back, the one who had been wild for him.

Hank scratched his stubbly chin, then gazed at Lenora's arm—hating its beauty.

"What are you thinking?" he asked.

"Do you need to penetrate my mind every second? I'm having *idle* goddamn thoughts."

Hank looked away. "Did you tell anyone what you're doing?"

"What?"

"The book."

"What about it?"

"Do they know you're stealing some poor woman's life?"

Lenora looked hurt for a second. It made her prettier. "Is that really what you think I'm doing?"

"Yes." He blinked at the white wall. "You're stealing her hell." He shook his head. "Because you've never been to hell— you wouldn't know how to describe it."

"I don't know. This feels a little like hell."

Hank imagined throwing something at the wall. Like a lamp or a chair. Just to change the look on her face. "You think you're so smart," he said.

"You think you're so *moral*."

"Does that woman know you'll disappear the *second* the book is done? Did you tell her that?"

"That woman's name is Angie. And who says I'll stop seeing her?"

"I know you." He trained his eyes on her. "You're a vampire." He went on staring, coating her with disgust. "It's why your books are so good—they're full of *actual* lives."

Lenora dropped her chin, stared at her legs.

Helplessly Hank joined her there.

"Do you think we love each other?" she asked.

He stiffened. "Why would you ask that?"

"Because I wonder."

"You *wonder*? But I say it all the time." He shook his head. "You mean do you love *me*. That's what you fucking wonder."

"I wonder about you too. You say it so much—like compulsively. You *need* it." Her gaze zapped coolly around the room. "That's not love."

"Well you wouldn't know, would you? Because you don't need anything . . . but fame."

Lenora had resumed staring at her legs.

"I miss you," he said. "I wish you missed me."

"How can I miss you when you won't go away?"

Hank blinked at her a moment. Then he went white, stormed off to the bathroom, shut the door and threw himself down on the blue bath mat. He had come there to sob but instead vomited a dark sauce like blood or chocolate. It seemed there would be more but he just knelt there panting with his chin on the toilet seat.

The room twitched and spun and he tried to remember what the fuck he had eaten. Then he closed his eyes and saw all

the little cheese cubes on toothpicks . . . a single cracker . . .
three grapes.

He wiped his mouth and curled like a comma on the rug.
He wanted to cry but couldn't. He slept.

In the morning birds chirped and one apart from the rest,
screaming a hideous tune. *One bird always sings alone,* he thought.
The one who can't sing—he sings alone. Hank unstuck his mouth
from the blue bath mat. Sunlight splashed into his eyes like
Clorox.

A few seconds rolled by and reality assembled itself. He
grasped his pounding forehead and remembered Lenora's face,
her smeary red mouth, the words: *How can I miss you when you
won't go away?*

In the mirror a creature blinked back at him. He ducked his
face over the sink and shocked it with cold water, massaging his
stubbly jaw. *How can I miss you when you won't go away?* The
phrase haunted his thoughts until it dawned on him: they were
lyrics from a Dan Hicks song.

Anger moved him like a windup toy to the kitchen, where
he paused in the doorframe to stare.

Lenora was smoking by the window, fanned-out papers and
a small brass ashtray before her on the round wood table. She
wore a pale orange silk robe patterned with silvery flowers, her
tangled brown hair beaming in sunshine.

"Dan Hicks," he said.

"What?"

"How can I miss you when you won't go away."

She stared.

"You fucking said that to me last night."

"Oh."

"It's the name of a Dan Hicks song."

"Okay."

He stared. "Are you even listening?"

She took a drag and the smoke seemed to vanish inside her. "My mom died," she said.

"What?"

"She fell."

"When did this happen?"

"This morning. They just called me."

"Shit."

Lenora made an O with her mouth, released a pale cloud. "There isn't enough time to impress people," she said.

"You wanted to impress her?"

"I think I did." She held very still with a pained look of contemplation. "I think I loved her."

"Of course you did."

"No—not *of course*," she said nastily. "You don't have to love your mother—a lot of people don't. Maybe *most* people don't. I thought I didn't . . . but I do." Her gaze flew around the room and crashed into his. "I loved her," she said. "And I don't love you."

Hank heard static. He held the doorframe, his fingertips fused to the wood. He could stand there forever, he thought, become part of the wall.

"Why would you say that?" he managed.

"It's what I'm thinking." She stabbed her cigarette out. "I thought you liked that."

"Liked *what*?"

"That I say what I'm thinking."

"I do—of course I do. But damn it . . . I wish you were thinking something else."

"I might go to Paris."

He stared. *I might chop your head off,* he thought.

"I just want to be alone."

"In the most romantic city in the world—that's repulsive, Lenora."

"Fine. It's repulsive."

Hank shut his eyes, listened to the pounding chamber of his poisoned body. He heard his heart—he thought he did. It sounded sick and broken, like a tin clock at the bottom of a murky pond, ticking somehow, one whiskered fish floating by.

Lenora slammed her fist down on the table and his eyes popped open.

"I should have known she would *fall*," she said.

"How could you have known?"

"You should've seen her. She looked so small in her nightgown. She had the skinny—almost *girlish* legs of a skeleton. And she kept asking to see her father," Lenora said, transfixed. "It's so weird—dementia. Everyone you ever cared about comes back to life."

"I know. It's like one big wish." Hank walked toward her, not knowing what he would do when he got there.

Lenora started to cry.

He took her head in his hands and stroked it, which felt absurd, tending to the woman who didn't love him anymore. But his love for her—it was intact.

A block of light trembled on the table, faintly pink. A merciful light.

Hank looked down at the mess of papers before her. "What is all this?"

"The contest." She sniffed. "The goddamn *stories*."

"Did you pick someone?"

"No." She wiped her nose. "People got less interesting the longer I looked."

George Harrison and the End of the World

George Harrison was a Pisces, she thought. *And I am a Capricorn.* She was in bed with her laptop balanced on her stomach. On the screen she read that some Pisces and Capricorn couples can make it work, but only if the Capricorn can learn to be less controlling. *I could be less controlling,* she thought, feeling certain.

But he was dead. It was like everything else. She was too late. *It's not the end of the world,* she imagined her father would say. Because her father always said this when someone was moping. *But it is,* she thought. *It's the end of the world.*

All day she had been trying to write. She was so close but she was also lost. She was crawling in the dark. She minimized the astrology love-match screen, then read the last page she had written with building disappointment.

"It's just a collection of stories," she said aloud. "You just have to finish the last story. Why is that so fucking hard?" Instantly she felt a slap of shame for talking to herself. She realized she was impersonating her father. It was a familiar shock that left her feeling hollow and used, like someone entered by a parasite that hooks into the brain and rides the body around like a car.

She shut her eyes tightly, then opened them wide. It was obvious why the story was hard to finish. Because it was about her. *And I hate myself,* she thought. It was no secret. Everyone in her life was always saying, "You have to love yourself." It made her hate them too.

She began scrolling through all the Beatles songs on her computer. Then she clicked on the most played song: "Here Comes the Sun," and the same sweet little guitar came into the room, the same voice. Instantly it threw her into ecstasy. *Little darling, it's been a long cold lonely winter. Little darling, it feels like years since it's been here.*

Her eyes filled with tears. She wondered how the same song continued to touch her this way. *It has all the same little fingers,* she thought, her eyes shimmering in the white glare of the screen. She sat up and a fat tear landed on the *R* key.

The Beatles wrote children's songs, she thought, wiping her eyes with the back of her hand. *And George wrote the weird ones. That's why I like him,* she decided. *Cause I'm a weird little girl.*

But she wasn't a little girl. She was twenty-eight, though it hardly seemed true. The thought shoved her into despair. *I'm not old yet,* she thought, frowning at the computer. *But I'm not young either.* She imagined two islands: one of babyhood, the other decrepitude. And she saw herself wading between them, seaweed flowing at her ankles. *I could drown this way,* she thought. *Between worlds.*

The song went on and the sweetness was crushing. She longed to fall into George Harrison's vulnerability—that yawning abyss. But she couldn't. She was too aware of how many seconds were left in the song: forty-six. Now it was forty-two. *Why does everything have to end?* she thought and paused the song in anger.

She moved her laptop to the foot of the bed and scratched her stomach. She wore just underwear and a T-shirt with an alligator on it. Out of habit she reached for the old record cover leaning against the wall by the bed: *Rubber Soul*. She didn't have a record player but she wanted one. The record had appeared one day on a tan blanket in the street. It sat between some scuffed VHS tapes and an ugly brown leather jacket. It was four dollars. "Is two okay?" she had asked the bearded man but he shook his head. "Four." So she gave him four.

Now she took the record into her hands and stared at it, moving her fingers over the four faces. When she reached George, she pulled her hand back. His cheek felt warm. Then she noticed he was blinking. He was staring at her.

Her heart raced. "It's you."

"Where am I?" His eyes zapped around the small pink room. Papers everywhere. A green bureau crowded with Coke cans. Cigarette butts pressed out on the windowsill. He seemed to clock each thing.

"In my—well, this is my room."

He stared a second. "Why am I here?"

"I don't know," she said but it felt like a lie. He seemed to be there because she had prayed for him to be. Because there was a God—a *good* God—the kind who returned phone calls.

For a while they just stared at each other. Then, cocking his head, he said, "You're so nervous."

"No I'm not," she said and he went on staring. It made her squirm. "I mean, maybe I'm a *little* nervous," she said. "About my book."

"What's wrong with it?"

"I have to finish the last story. And I can't."

"What's it about?"

"It's about me . . . and actually you're in it too."

"So it should be easy."

"But it isn't!"

"Maybe because you have to—"

"I know, I know," she interrupted, rolling her eyes. "I have to *love* myself."

George laughed. "No," he said.

"No?"

"No."

"I don't have to love myself?"

"No. You have to play."

"What—like a guitar?"

"No. You've got to have fun, that's all."

"Oh."

"At some point play got banished," he said in a rehearsed sort of way, like a monk had told him and he remembered. "Children play because they live in their own time. But most people when they get older, they *leave* their own time."

"Where do they go?"

"Wherever the culture tells them to."

"I don't understand."

"Play gets replaced with a desire to be accepted, a desire for *identity*," he sneered. "Everyone wants to *be* someone."

"It's easy for you," she said, feeling hurt. "You never had to be someone. You just *were* someone."

"How would you know?" He sucked his teeth. "You don't know me. You think wanting to fuck me means you know me?"

"Yes."

"It doesn't," he said with disgust. "You're a fantasy addict."

"I'm a writer," she shot back.

"So write then. Tell the truth."

She shook her head. "I can't. I don't know how." She was holding back a sob. "I'm always gonna be like this."

"Like what?"

"A monster."

George stared, his dark eyes softening. "So write about that."

The walls were glowing—pinker suddenly—like a sunset in the womb.

"What if no one cares?" she said. She couldn't imagine anything worse.

"Don't think so much about the future."

"Why the hell not?"

"*Because*," he said carefully, "it doesn't belong to you."

"Okay," she said. She was starting to feel a little angry. She pulled a cigarette from the pack on her side table and lit up. "So what *does* belong to me? Nothing? I've got nothing, right?"

"No. Not nothing. Come on. Not nothing."

"What then?" she said, smoke charging from her nostrils.

"You have this," he said. "*Today*. Not tomorrow."

She ashed onto the floor. "I'm not stupid."

"I know that," he said and a train of red hearts floated by. She touched one and it laughed in transit, then vanished.

"But am I crazy?" she asked.

"Yes," he grinned. Then all around the room she saw it towering in giant black letters, the word: YES. YES. *YES*.

She dragged on her cigarette and exhaled, then felt her cheeks warm up and wanted badly to be kissed.

"Give me a puff, will you?" he said and she held the cigarette to his lips. He took a long suck, then blew a skinny cloud. "Again," he said and she returned the cigarette to his mouth. He seemed to take all the time in the world inhaling. It felt religious. Then smoke poured from his mouth in a slow, sensual manner, crawling up through the air like a herd of lazy white lizards.

"Alright," he said and she dropped the cigarette in an old glass of water by the bed. Hearing it sizzle, she said, "I'm just a slow writer."

"Who needs to play," he smirked.

"What I need is quiet." She felt a speech gathering in her thoughts and contained it. "I'm not gonna talk about my process," she said, shaking her head. "It's too boring. I mean, I *hate* when writers talk about their process. They always look so proud of what they're saying, like it's the frosting on the cake."

"But it's the shit on the shoe."

"Right!" she exclaimed, then stared into his dark grin. It was a face both warlike and unprotected, which was exactly what she wanted from a man: something open and shut.

"Why am I in the story?" he asked.

"I don't know. Cause I can't stop thinking about you." She blinked thoughtfully. "If I'm gonna write about myself, I have to write about you. You're in my head." She stared hard at him. He didn't seem to mind. *He must be used to it,* she thought, which felt a little sad. Like he was a very special monkey.

"In the story you're dying of cancer and you've kind of accepted it," she explained. "You keep saying how everyone turns to dust and stuff like that. But I'm going nuts. I don't want you to die. I'm sitting by your hospital bed and I keep saying *it isn't fair, it isn't fair.*"

"What isn't fair?"

"That you're dying!" She stared at him, timid suddenly. "I mean, that you *died*. How could that be fair? All sorts of schmucks live to be a hundred . . . so they know something you'll never know."

George was quiet. A soft look of violation passed over his face.

The dead are innocent, she thought, feeling guilty. But she couldn't stop herself. "I just think I would've known how to touch you."

"You and every other girl in the world."

"Yeah well, every other girl is wrong. Every girl but me." She sat there staring and felt like a baby, then a fool, then a crazy person. "You're a creature of another time . . . a time I'd like to crawl into." She began to cry. "I can't be young now. I don't know how. But I could've been young then."

He just stared. Maybe he didn't agree that the sixties would've embraced her. She herself couldn't be entirely sure. But it was a feeling and it burned, the feeling of aloneness in her own time.

"How old do you think I am?" she asked, wiping her eyes.

"I don't know," he said. "Twenty?"

"Actually I'm twenty-eight," she beamed.

"*No,*" he said, grinning in his handsome, ghoulish way. "Really?"

"Really," she said seriously because it was a serious thing. "Twenty-*eight*."

"Well," he said, "you're doing an honor to your decade." Then he leaned out of the record cover as if it were a car window and kissed her on the mouth.

She heard saxophones and seagulls, a hammer hitting a nail. Everything in the world; everything holy and good. It was a wet, biting kiss and it stirred the glittering feeling in her crotch. Soon every cell in her body was glittering too. She hoped it would go on and on and on and somehow lead to sex. But his lips released her and he sank back into the record cover.

The spit he left on her tongue tasted like black tea and tobacco. There was a third element also, one that began quietly, but soon it was all she could taste. It was the surprising flavor of his flesh itself. Smiling, she thought, *No animal tastes alike.*

"God," she said, her eyes immense. "I like you so much. I might even love you."

"Why?" he asked, staring in his deadpan way.

Then a number rose in his eyes: 2,898,787,775. It was the number of women who loved him and it blazed a sickly yellow.

"What is it?" he asked.

"I don't know," she said quickly. "I didn't think you'd ask *why.*"

"Come on. Tell me."

"I like your visions. They make me wet. 'I Me Mine'—that song makes me *wet.* I wish you weren't George Harrison. I wish you were . . ." She touched the bone of his cheek. "I wish you were anyone."

"Anyone?"

"I wish you just like, worked at a deli."

"No." He moved his face from her hand. "You wouldn't want me then."

"Oh but I would! I would see you and I would just *know* you were wonderful. I would try to seduce you."

"What would you do?"

"I would walk up to the counter."

"And then?"

"You would say hello."

"And then?"

"I would say hello. I would just stand there."

"Enticing."

"No there's more."

"I'm listening."

"I would buy you a pickle."

He laughed.

"Or whatever you wanted. It would be like when someone at a bar buys the bartender a drink."

She was getting excited and the air knew it. God knew it. Even the little brown spiders in the walls knew and they didn't scare her. Not now, not tonight.

"Then I would invite you over," she continued. "I would bring you to this room and we would crawl onto the bed. I would kiss you but like where no one else has ever kissed you."

"Where?"

"Your eyelids." She smiled. "Your ass."

"Lots of people have kissed my ass," he smirked.

"No I mean *really* kiss your ass. Like with my mouth."

"I know what you meant."

"Well I would do it differently," she smiled. "And I would get completely naked. I would even take off my earrings and like if I was wearing lipstick I would rub it off with a Kleenex. Then I would lie on my back and I would open my vagina with my fingers," she said seriously. "And in there you would find the whole universe."

"The whole universe is in there?"

"Yeah."

"I've always wanted to see that."

"Wait, you've always wanted to see *what*?"

"Everything."

"Me too. That's why I can't sleep."

"You want a lot."

"I do." She leaned nearer to the record, to the wet heat of his breath.

"If I saw between your legs," he said, "what would I see? What does the whole universe look like?"

"I don't know. I think of infinity. The blackness of space."

"I think of a big yellow field and a little horse walks by."

"A little baby horse?"

"It's a baby, yeah."

"I love that . . . I guess the universe is vast so you have to pick something to look at."

He stared. "You haven't really told me—I want you to tell me *exactly* . . . why you want me."

She stared back. He seemed so insecure—more insecure than George Harrison had to be. *Maybe that is all a rock song is,* she thought. *Discomfort. Horrible embarrassment. Set to a tune.*

"C'mon," he said. *"Why?"*

"It's just something that happened. I woke up one day—I woke up burning," she said, loving the words. There was nothing better, nothing more electric than thinking something and saying it immediately. "Have you ever burned, George?"

"Yes."

"Is it hard to burn for people when everyone's burning for you?"

"Exactly. I can't match them. I can't even come *close.*" He looked away. "In the early days on tour when all the girls were screaming, I couldn't hear the band. I couldn't even hear my own voice—just all these screaming girls, you know."

"It's like *they* were the band—the screaming girls."

He laughed and she looked away, smiling uncontrollably. "I love the way you sing," she said. "I love that I can hear all the spit in your mouth . . . there's a hiss." Then, returning her eyes to his, she said, "You wrote all my favorite Beatles songs."

"*Oh,*" he grinned.

Blushing, she muttered, "I have to pee," and took the record with her to the bathroom. She leaned it up against the green tile wall, then pulled her underwear down and sat on the toilet.

"Nice music," George said as she peed. He laughed and she joined in, quite hysterically. Then she looked at the other three Beatles, who remained flat and devoid of animation. They looked spooky next to George's breathing face, like deer heads on a wall.

She flushed and shut the toilet, then sat cross-legged on the cold tile floor, slouching before the record. "There's such sadness in you," she said.

"No that's you."

She frowned. "That's just the problem. I can't see what's inside anyone."

"Well," he laughed, "we aren't frogs in your laboratory."

She smiled sadly. "I know. I just . . . I can't connect with anyone. I always think I know what someone's face is saying," she said, shaking her head. "And I'm always wrong." She looked down at her naked toes on the green tile floor. "I'm so intense. I repulse people."

"I'm telling you, you need to play."

"Stop saying that. It's like you have one idea." She touched her forehead and grimaced. "I'm sorry," she said. "I just have to finish this story. Then I'll calm down."

"No," he said. "There will always be another story. You will never be calm."

Suddenly he looked exactly like the devil. And she knew he

was right. The story loomed, unfinished, one of a lifetime of stories. It was enough to make her scream.

"In the story we're talking," she said anxiously. "Kind of like we're talking right now. Only something happens."

"What happens?"

"Well I don't know. That's the problem."

"Does something have to happen?"

"Yes," she said and waited for him to make a suggestion. But he didn't. "What do you think should happen?" she asked. "I mean, what do you think *would* happen? I want it to feel, you know, *real*."

"What about this?"

"This now?"

He nodded.

She stared at him a minute, then picked up the record and walked swiftly back to her bed. There she began typing all the words that had passed between them, all the ones she could remember.

Afterward she read over what she had written. She wasn't sure if it was any good. "God damn," she said.

"What?" George said. The record was lying flat beside her.

"I just feel like such an idiot sometimes."

"Well everyone's an idiot *sometimes*."

She laughed, then stared into space. "Maybe ambition is the great distraction . . . cause it just makes you greedy."

"Everyone is greedy. Everyone is exactly the same."

She blinked. *Maybe George Harrison is crazy,* she thought, then reached for the phone. It was heavy and pea green, a rotary phone from the sixties.

As it rang she held her breath. She always did this. She could never breathe until the human at the other end put a stop to all the ringing—said hello. She decided then—waiting for it—that it was the most romantic word: hello.

The ringing ceased. She heard her father but not his hello. He just breathed directly into the phone—into her ear. He always did this.

"Dad?"

"Saundra, it's very late."

"I know—I'm sorry. I have to ask you something."

"Are you alright?"

"I'm fine."

"What have you done? Have you *done* something?"

"Daddy, I'm writing. And I think this could be good—like really, *really* good—but I'm not sure."

"Well," he yawned, "it's usually a spell, Saundra—the good feeling."

"I know that."

"You can't *really* see a sentence until you feel bad again."

"Yes, I know."

"Good."

She imagined him touching his mustache as he always did—compulsively.

"You had a question?"

"Yes."

"Go ahead."

She sat up, straightening her spine as if he were there, watching. "Are there any fables or stories where a woman opens her vagina and inside is the whole universe?"

He was quiet.

"I'm writing a story where that happens," she said. "I need to know if I'm writing a story that has already been written."

"Well all stories—"

"Yeah, yeah, they've all been written—I *know*. But has the universe ever shown up in a woman's vagina?"

"All the time. Why just yesterday—"

"Daddy, I'm serious."

"Well what do you mean by the whole universe?"

"I mean the birds, the trees, the entire solar system—everything. The universe, Daddy. The *universe*."

"Well there's a scene in an Almodóvar movie where a man walks into a woman's vagina and it's enormous. But it's not the universe."

"Okay."

"And there's an Italo Calvino story where the whole universe is a woman's fat arms and breasts. But not her vagina."

"Okay."

"And then there's the Courbet painting of the vagina called *L'Origine du monde*. But it's not *L'Origine du universe*."

He laughed and then she laughed. They laughed together heartily.

"You know I was sleeping, Saundra."

"I'm sorry. I had to know. I knew you would know."

He was silent. A pleased silence, she thought.

"You should work in the vagina," she said. "Like at the front desk of one . . . answer absurd questions like mine all day."

"I think I've worked in several."

She smiled and knew that he was also smiling. It was a weird smile, his was—a secret smile, one obscured by mustache hairs.

On the pink wall a brown spider made its diagonal dash. A second one followed, then a third and she wondered if an egg had hatched. She didn't care. She lay there with the phone in her hand, basking in something like sunshine. It was the infinite weirdness of the world and it made her smile again, with her father smiling on the other line, the weirdest man. And she the weirdest woman. And George, blinking beside her, the weirdest Beatle.

"Good night, Saundra," her father said.

She waited for his phone to hit the cradle and imagined him in his navy robe, shuffling back to bed. She saw him part the sheets and enter them. She hung up.

"How can you say vagina to your father?" George asked.

"I don't know. I just can. He's a professor of German literature."

"Oh."

"I can't do anything that normal people can," she grinned. "But I can do everything they *can't*."

George laughed.

"He's not always so nice—my dad. He can be very cruel out of nowhere."

"But you keep calling him. Even though he can be cruel."

"Even though." She picked the record up and looked into his eyes. "I think I'm afraid to finish the book," she said. "Like finishing the book means death." She sighed. "I don't wanna die."

"You won't," he said. "Your book isn't you."

"What about your music? Was that you?"

"No. It was just something I did."

She glanced at her cigarette pack and decided not to reach for it. She said, "What's it like anyway, dying?"

"It's like nothing," he said evenly. "Nothing at all."

She peered at him. "What the hell does that mean?"

"You'll see. It's like nothing. We really die . . . I did."

What he said made her stomach hurt. He had died and not

even God could change that. *Especially not God,* she thought. He was gone, long gone. And the face she was staring into was her own.

She put the record down and returned her eyes to the computer, then unpaused "Here Comes the Sun" and fell back into the song, its tender grip. There were only thirty-two seconds left. Now it was twenty-six. *It'll be over soon,* she thought, the seconds vanishing forever. *It's ending now,* she thought. *This is the end.*